Three Cursing Birds

AXEL HATCHETT MYSTERY VOL. 4

Steven LeRoy Nelson

BLOOD AND THUNDER PRESS

BLOOD AND THUNDER PRESS
3612 Sheffield Lane
Colorado Springs, CO 80907
www.bloodandthunderpress.com

ISBN: 1940469031
ISBN-13: 978-1-940469-03-4

To my little gooseberry tart.

1

little after midnight my phone rang. I didn't want to blind myself by turning on any lights, so I groped my way to the living room.

"Axe speaking," I said into the phone. "You interrupted my beauty sleep. Call back when I'm beautiful." I hung up. If it was important, they'd call back. It was very early Sunday morning, cold out, and just a few days before Christmas.

I lit a cigar. The phone rang again.

"Yeah?"

"Axe? This is Eben." Ah, Dr. Mulford, retired professor of British literature, and a friend.

"Hey, Eben. Who let you stay up this late?"

"I need a favor. Can you meet me at Quartz Quarry General?"

That woke me up.

"You're not hurt, are you?"

"No, it's a friend of mine, a former colleague — Dr. Kirsten Lund. A couple of ruffians attacked her at her house tonight and pushed her out of an upstairs' window. She sustained a broken leg."

"Ruffians, huh? So, do you need a shoulder to cry on, or my services as a detective?"

"I can cry on my own shoulder. I need you to help me talk Kirsten into hiring you. At present she considers the idea silly."

"She'll have to get over that. Listen, where are you now?"

"At the hospital. Kirsten's room."

"Give me the room number. I'll get there as soon as I can."

I hung up, climbed into my clothes, and even shaved a little. Then I slicked down my hair. No point in making a bad impression on a prospective client. I fired up my red Nash and chugged to the hospital. This time of night I pretty much had the roads to myself. The sky was clear and the moon made the trees cast zebra-stripe shadows across the snow-dusted streets.

Eben was waiting for me in his friend's room. There was a snoring sleeper in the other bed. Dr. Lund was lying in the bed closest to the door, her head raised on a stack of pillows. A spanking new cast adorned one long leg. She was beautiful — a Nordic queen — with her long blonde hair shot with silver. She had high cheekbones and delicate features. The wind and sun hadn't done any favors to her skin though. She might have been fifty, and I couldn't help wondering what she'd looked like ten years earlier.

Eben stood up, shook my hand. "Thanks for coming, old man."

Always with the old man stuff. Eben was seventy to my thirty-six. He was normally a dapper little guy, but not tonight. His shirt wasn't tucked in all the way, his tie was badly knotted, and he wore house slippers instead of shoes.

"Axe," he said, "this is my friend and colleague, Kirsten Lund. Kirsten, this is the detective friend I told you about. Axel Hatchett."

We mumbled our hellos.

"How'd you get in this fix?" I asked her.

"Breaking a leg wasn't part of my Christmas plans. But let me say right now, I'm in no way interested in hiring a private investigator."

"Fair enough. But I'd still like to hear your story. I got out of bed and came over here just to hear it."

"There's nothing to tell, really. Nothing important. Just some prank that went too far."

"If you won't tell him, then I will," said Eben.

She gave him a sharp look with her steel-gray eyes.

"I was dangled out a window by two masked thugs, and they dropped me. It was an accident, I think. My house is two-and-a-half stories. I rent out the bottom floor, and the upper floor is my living space. I've turned the attic into an office and workshop."

"Workshop? But you're a professor."

She smiled, almost wistfully.

"Yes. The workshop's for my hobby. I'm a wood carver. Not a very good one, I'm afraid, but I love it."

"How is it that two guys dangled you out of a window? Was it an attic window?"

"It was. I fell about twenty feet or so." She shuddered, remembering. "They wanted something from me, and I wouldn't give it to them."

"What did they want exactly?'

"A carving. An ivory ibis."

"What's an ibis? Some kind of bird?"

"That's a good guess. This one was a sacred Egyptian ibis, carved from ivory."

"Oh? Worth a lot?"

"No, but there's a story behind it."

"Sounds like I'll want to hear that story. Tell me about the ivory ibis."

"It all started in ancient Egypt."

"Sure it did."

She gave me a dirty look. "Are you familiar, Mr. Hatchett, with Egyptian mythology, or religion?"

"No. It's not really in my line," I admitted.

"Then you don't know about the god, Thoth. He had a human body and the head of a bird He was the Egyptian god of knowledge, writing, and wisdom."

"Huh. God of knowledge—so he was sort of a professor like you and Eben." That made them both laugh. "Sounds like an easy guy to spot, especially in a Hawaiian shirt."

4

"No doubt. Have you ever heard about King Tut's tomb, discovered and opened in the nineteen twenties?"

"Sure, everybody knows about that. All that stuff's in a museum now. It's worth a fortune."

"Its archeological value is immeasurable. Anyway, about the same time that King Tut's tomb was found, another, lesser, tomb was broken into. The thief, for that is exactly what he was, was being followed by other thieves. His life was in danger. He had only enough time to fill a sack full of choice artifacts and flee the scene. He later made a detailed map so he would be able to return to the tomb later. That's the story."

"You don't believe it?"

"I have my doubts. I'm not an Egyptologist, obviously, though I do teach mythology courses. It sounds like a typical lost treasure tale. Most of them aren't true, but people love hearing them and repeating them."

"Sure, we all get a kick out of that sort of thing."

"Yes. According to the rest of the tale, the thief worked at the time in a museum somewhere. These stories are always vague. There was a display of Egyptian artifacts in the museum. Well, this man, whose name might have been Appleton, or Stapleton, or something else, needed a place to hide his treasure map. One of the items taken from the tomb was an ivory ibis. Its base was hollow — perhaps naturally, since it was carved from a hippopotamus tooth.

"He copied the map in fine print on a thin roll of paper, stuffed it into the base of the ibis, then capped the hole with a piece of artificially-aged ivory. Then he slipped the figure in among the museum's Egyptian display.

"According to the legend, not long afterwards, the man was found murdered in his bed. He'd been tortured by having the bottoms of his feet burned. And after his death his killers wrapped him up like a mummy, using strips torn from his bed sheets."

"Quite a colorful tale, Dr. Lund, and a creepy one."

"It gets better. Whoever killed Appleton—or whatever his name was—must have failed to force him to reveal the location of the map. The ivory ibis remained in the museum for years afterwards."

"Don't tell me. It was eventually stolen."

"It was, along with a lot of other items. The ivory ibis has resurfaced several times, but without its hidden map being discovered. The story further states that there is a curse attached to the figure. Whoever possesses it ends up dying, usually in a horrible fashion. The ibis has changed hands many times, and has left a trail of dead owners behind it."

"OK. If you don't mind my asking, why are you telling me this story?"

She frowned—a displeased Viking queen.

"First, because you asked me to. Second, because I am the current owner of the ibis. The men who dropped me out of my attic window were trying to get me to tell them where it is."

"You mean this carved bird actually exists?"

"In a manner of speaking, yes. There are actually three of them. Let me explain. I have a colleague, an archeologist named Dr. Ollie Crampton. He travels quite a bit, mostly in the southwestern United States. About a year ago, he came across the first ivory ibis in a used furniture store in New Mexico. You never know what you're going to find in such places. He bought it and brought it to me as a gift. He's the one who told me the story of the treasure map. He'd first heard it years before, from a fellow archeologist.

"Dr. Crampton thought the tale was amusing, and he believed I might be interested in the carved figure since I like to carve similar art pieces. In my workshop I have quite a collection of exotic woods, and even some pieces of ivory. People are always giving me such things that they've picked up here and there.

"At that time I had two walrus tusks my sister had picked up on a trip to Alaska. I was saving them for something special. I ended up carving two copies of the ivory ibis Ollie had given me. I then gave the original figure to our little museum."

"The college has a museum?"

"Yes. It's pathetic, really, but it's all we've got. I

kept one of the copies for myself and gave Ollie the other one. As I said, this was about a year ago."

"But there wasn't any treasure map stuffed into the base of the figure your friend gave you?"

"No. The base appeared solid. But I did a rather amusing thing. I couldn't help thinking about the silly tale of the map leading to a hidden tomb in Egypt. About six months ago I fell down the stairs in my home. Clumsy of me. I guess I was just wool-gathering and wasn't watching what I was doing. Anyway, I knew I'd have to go to the hospital because my wrist swelled up like a balloon. It turned out to be broken."

"You need to take better care of yourself," said Eben. "Really, you're quite heedless sometimes."

"My dear Eben, we all break bones. I figured that since I was going to have to have x-rays, I might as well take the ivory ibis with me to the hospital and see if I could talk them into x-raying it for me. Silly really, but they were very cooperative. They x-rayed my wrist and the figurine at the same time. The base of the figure was not hollow. There was no map inside. I was unreasonably disappointed."

"Is that when you gave it to the museum?"

"Yes."

"And now it's been stolen," said Eben. "About a week or so ago. The curator, who is also our librarian, noticed the figure was gone one morning when he was checking the collection. Nothing else was taken."

"How did the thief manage to break in?" I asked.

Dr. Lund snorted. "The museum is located in an old storeroom off of the library. You could probably pick the lock with a bobby pin."

"I see. And the curator—the librarian— informed you of the theft?"

"Yes. He was quite upset. I didn't really care that much, but it puzzled me. I talked to Eben about it and we both wondered if someone had heard the legend and decided to take it seriously."

"That is correct," said Eben. "We laughed about it. But it is no laughing matter now."

"Let's see if I've got this straight," I said. "Somebody heard the story about the ivory ibis and decided to check to see if it was true. So this person stole it from the museum and probably broke it open and discovered there was no map inside. But they'd heard that you'd carved a couple of copies of the dingus, and they might have thought that you'd given the museum one of the copies and kept the original for yourself. Maybe they figured you were going to look for the treasure on your own. Or, they might have believed you didn't know about the map hidden in the ibises' innards. Who knows?

"Whatever they were thinking, they came to your house and tried to scare you into giving them the right ibis. You refused to cooperate and they decided to dangle you out of an upstairs' window

9

STEVEN LEROY NELSON

to get you to talk. Then they accidently dropped
you. Fortunately, you only broke a leg instead of
breaking your neck. Is that about right?"

"Yes, except for one thing. The thieves were at
my house when I came home tonight. I'd been at-
tending a friend's Christmas party. In my absence
the two men had broken into my place and torn it
apart looking for the figurine."

"Why couldn't they find it?"

"They looked in all the wrong places. I'd recently decided to give it as a Christmas gift to a colleague of mine who'd always admired it. I'd already wrapped it up in Christmas paper and put it
under the pathetic little Christmas tree I have in
my living room. I was planning to have the Snelfs
over for Christmas."

"The Snelfs?"

"Raymond and Cassandra. Ray is an English
prof, like me, and an old friend. He loves the story
of the ivory ibis."

"Here's a question for you. When these two
guys were hanging you out of your attic window,
why didn't you just tell them where the ibis was?
Why didn't you just give it to them?"

She raised up on her stack of pillows and flared
her delicate nostrils.

"I wouldn't give them the satisfaction."

"Kirsten's always been very stubborn," Eben
whispered to me. "Viking blood, you know."

"Besides," said Lund, "if I gave them the bird
they might have hurt me."

"I think they did," I said.

"Yes, but accidently. As long as I don't cooperate with them they'll need me alive."

"You don't actually think they'd kill you, do you?"

"How would I know? I don't know who they are. They obviously think I have in my possession a map leading to a fortune in Egyptian artifacts. Greed brings out the worst in people. And, if I gave them the thing, they'd just break it and discover that there's no map in it. Then they'd come after me again."

"Maybe you're right, but it sounds loopy to me. You said there was a third one of these ivory figures. You gave it to your friend — Ollie, was it? Have you warned him?"

"He's on sabbatical, on a dig."

"This time of year?"

"Yes, in southern New Mexico. It's much warmer down there than it is here. Besides, he wouldn't let a little cold stop him. He's an iron man."

"Is he married? Is there anybody in his house while he's away?"

"No, he's not married. A friend, a colleague, is staying in his place while he's gone. I had Eben try calling her earlier, but she didn't answer the phone."

"I'll try again," said Eben. "If I can't reach her, I'll try going over to her place. Or, Ollie's place. I'll leave a note on her door if she's not there. This is terrible. The whole situation is awful. I wish the police had agreed to guard your hospital room."

"It's all right," said Kirsten. "No one's going to bother me here, except the nurses and their damned shots."

"Speaking of which," said Eben, "do you think it might be time for more morphine? You look pained."

"I'm fine, only aggravated. A broken leg! I already hate this cast. I'll be wearing it for weeks."

"It can't be helped," said Eben. "I'll visit you as often as you want, and bring you books."

"I wish you could bring me my carving tools. I don't suppose the doctors would allow that."

"Certainly not. In your condition you might slip and cut yourself. Give me a list of the books you'd like."

"Oh, anything. Bring me Homer — he always cheers me up. As for you, Eben, you need to go home, get some sleep. Thank you for everything. You've been a saint. I'm glad I called you."

"Who's the dame staying at your friend Ollie's place?" I asked.

"Dame?" Kirsten flared her nostrils again. "Dr. Lilith Umbrey. Professor of British literature."

"Sure. She needs to be warned. Will she know where the bird is, the copy you gave your archeologist friend?"

"It was on Ollie's mantel for the longest time. I don't know why it wouldn't still be there. Ollie will be back right after the holidays. He always avoids Christmas in Quartz Quarry if he can. His family, you know. I could write to him, but he's not that good at keeping up with his mail. Still, I don't know why he'd move the bird."

"We'll check with Dr. Umbrey," I said.

"Really, I think it's time we left," said Eben. "You need rest, poor Kirsten. Axe and I are just bothering you with our questions."

"Take my key," she told him. "Check my place. It's a mess. But check to make sure the ibis is still under the Christmas tree. If it is, take it. Put it someplace safe. I won't give those thieves the satisfaction of getting their hands on it."

"Yes," said Eben. "We'll check your place and warn Minnie if she's there. We'll take the carving. We'll drop by Lilith's house and warn her, or leave a note."

"Take Ollie's ibis too. Hide them both. I want these thieves stymied."

"If you think that's wise," said Eben. He looked at me.

"I don't think it's wise," I said. "Let them have the damned birds. They'll leave you alone then."

"No, they won't." said Lund. "They won't be satisfied until they have that map, and it doesn't exist."

"Maybe you could make up a fake map," I said. "Send the hoodlums off to Egypt on a wild goose chase."

She smiled, showing off white, even, teeth. "That's actually an excellent idea," said Lund.

"But I don't know enough about Egypt, and the pyramids, to draw up a convincing map. Maybe someone at the college could, but it would take time. I guess I could make some phone calls. Is there a phone in this room?"

"There is," said Eben. "But don't worry yourself about such things right now. Get some sleep."

About then a black-haired nurse in a white starched uniform came in and gave Lund an injection.

"This will help you sleep," the nurse told her.

"It's time we were going," said Eben. "I'll check on you later, Kirsten. I'll come see you, and I'll bring a copy of Homer."

"Thanks, Eben. I'm sorry I dragged you out of bed so late."

"No bother, really. I'm always happy to see you, Kirsten. I'm only sorry for the circumstances. Do what the nurses tell you to do. I'll check on you later." He reached out a small hand and barely caressed one of Lund's cheeks. We left the hospital room and I headed toward the elevators.

2

"Let's take the stairs," said Eben. "A man of my sedentary ways needs all the exercise he can get."

I shrugged and we found the stairwell and headed down. Eben didn't speak until we'd reached the lobby, and he hummed a little tune under his breath to keep me from starting any conversation. We walked out of Quartz Quarry General and started across the parking lot.

"We'll take my car," said Eben. "It's just over here. No point in taking both our cars. Crampton's house and Kirsten's house are in the same neighborhood, not far from here. I'll bring you back to the hospital to pick up your vehicle when we're finished with our visits. That is—you're coming with me?"

"Wouldn't miss it."

"Thank you. I'd like to hire you to investigate Kirsten's attack. Are you presently engaged in a case?"

"As it happens, no. But why should you hire me? Let Lund retain me if she wants."

"That's the problem. You heard what she said. She thinks the idea of hiring a detective is ridiculous. I don't agree."

"Then I'll do the job for free, as a favor to you."

"Nonsense. I hear you're going to be married soon. Think of your future wife."

"OK. But I insist on giving you a discount. That's my last word."

"You're as stubborn as Kirsten."

"But not as beautiful."

"Few people are. Here's my car. I just traded my Hillman for it. What do you think?"

He stopped in front of a car about the size and shape of a bump in the road. In the night light it looked white, but I think it might have been a pale green. It was one of those little German rollerskates, a Volkswagen. I'd heard of them, but this was my first introduction to the actual animal.

"You're going to have a damned hard time finding parts for this thing when it breaks down," I said. "Assuming you keep it that long."

"I have expectations that the brand will prove popular. However, I've been wrong before."

We pretzeled ourselves into the little machine and Eben drove off to start our new adventure.

"A cold winter's night," I said, rubbing my gloved hands together.

"Yes. 'St. Agnes Eve—Ah, bitter chill it was! The owl, for all his feathers, was a-cold: the hare limped trembling through the frozen grass, and silent was the flock in wooly fold.'"

"You damned professors and your damned quotes," I grumbled. "Still, I liked that part about the trembling bunny. What do you know about this ivory bird business that I haven't already heard?"

"Little, if anything. The story was quite popular around the college for a time, so I hear. No one took it seriously. I can't imagine who's behind Kirsten's attack."

"Maybe a couple of starving college students."

"Possibly. But if they're starving, how could they hope to gather the funds necessary to travel to Egypt and incur the expense of initiating a treasure hunt?"

"Good point."

"You haven't any other ideas?"

"Hey, we're just getting started."

"Yes, but I have great confidence in your agile detective's mind."

"Well, since you mention it, I do have one idea. Ever hear of an eccentric fellow named Crosby Dumpler?"

"No. I'd remember the name. Who is he, a treasure hunter?"

"In his spare time, yes. He's a dentist. Pretty well fixed, I imagine. He has a cute little wife who he's always suspecting of stepping out on him. He's hired me a couple of times to follow her around."

"And? Does the lady have a roving eye?"

"If she does, it doesn't go any farther than that. No clandestine meetings at motels on the edge of town. No office flirtations—she works as a nurse in an old folks' home. I could never find anything against her."

"And what has this to do with treasure hunting?"

"Don't be so impatient. I'm getting to that. I like talking to my clients; I learn all kinds of things. I got Dumpler talking about his private life. A few years ago he heard this story about a lost gold mine up in the Foggy Top Mountains. You familiar with them?"

"Of course. On clear days I can see the Foggy Tops from my own kitchen window. You ought to know that."

"I just wanted to see if you were still listening. As the story goes, an old prospector discovered what was rumored to be a fat vein of almost pure gold, but he was also a religious nut. For every hundred pounds or so of gold he dug out of the mountains, he'd set aside a few pounds to make a statue out of. He set up his own smelting operation, and he was a bit of a frustrated artist.

"He ended up making a bunch of gold statues. The first one was Jehovah himself. Then Jesus. Then Mary. Even the Holy Ghost. I'd like to see what that one looked like. He kept finding gold, so he started fashioning gold saints. There were a total of twenty such figures. You can imagine what they'd be worth."

"A pretty penny, as they say. What did he do with them?"

"He lined them up in a low-ceilinged cave somewhere, also in the Foggy Tops. It was his own private religious shrine. No one had ever seen it but the miner himself. Anyway, his mine finally played out. He was getting up in years by then. He moved to town, set up in a nice mansion, and managed to go through most of his money before he died. Over the years, he told the tale of the gold saints — not to mention the holy family — to a few friends, but he never revealed to anyone where the statues were located."

"And then he died, of course, and left no map."

"No, he did leave a map. It was found inside the belly of a stuffed burro, a favorite of the old miner's. The burro was donated to the Quartz Quarry Historical Museum. It was a little moth-eaten, and when they went to refurbish it, they discovered the map. The son of the museum curator spent some time looking for the treasure, but apparently the miner had become dotty by the time he drew the thing, so the landmarks were all mixed up, or nonexistent. The son finally sold the map. It got sold a few more times, over the years, and my client, Crosby Dumpler, finally came into possession of it."

"Fascinating. What was the name of the burro?"

"Isolde. Why?"

"I'm attempting to emulate your investigative

techniques. You've often mentioned how the tiniest of details can prove invaluable in the solving of a crime."

"Yeah, I know, I've heard myself talk. But if the name of that stuffed burro turns out to be the key to solving the ivory ibis case, I'll buy you a new snake." My friend Eben has what I consider a depraved interest in serpents, and he owns several of the slimy things.

"I'll hold you to that, Axe. A green mamba would be a welcome addition to my little zoo."

"Sure. Sometimes you give me the willies, Eben. Anyhow, getting back to my story. The dentist bought the map and tried his luck at finding the statues."

"He failed, no doubt."

"He didn't. He found a partner who was something of a cave enthusiast. He liked to crawl around in them"

"A spelunker."

"And how. He knew of a lot of caves in the Foggy Top Mountains, and explored quite a few of them. And he thought he might have some ideas about where the old miner's religious display could be found. Apparently, there are some caves up there that aren't very stable. The stalactites tend to fall down onto the spelunker's heads. Some of the more dangerous caverns have even been sealed up to keep people out of them."

"I'm impressed you know a big word like 'stalactite.' Perhaps I've underestimated your education."

"Just drive, will you? How much farther?"

"We're almost there. It's the same neighbor-hood where I live. Most of the professors live in that one old neighborhood that surrounds the college campus. Go on with your story."

"The dentist's partner thought the gold figures might be buried under a bunch of debris. They searched for a couple of years. And then, one bright morning, they found the gold religious dinguses."

"It wouldn't have been a bright morning inside a cave."

"It was bright outside. There weren't actually twenty statues; there were only three. God, his Son, and Mother Mary. And the miner hadn't really been much of an artist. In fact, Jesus and Mary looked an awful lot alike, and Jehovah looked like one of the Seven Dwarves. But they were big, and solid gold.

"The things were so heavy that the treasure hunters knew they couldn't pack them out on their backs, so they went back to town and hired a sturdy mule and led it as close to the cave as they could get. Then they carried the statues, one at a time, to the waiting mule. When they finally got back to town, they tucked the treasure away in the dentist's garage.

"But here's the part of the story I like best. A couple of weeks later, the spelunker got the idea of going back to the cave and digging around some more just in case they'd overlooked other statues. Of course, he took the dentist with him, and that's when it happened. The spelunker fell down into a deep pit and broke his neck."

"Tragic. So he never got to enjoy his share of the treasure."

"No. Here's the punch line. The dead man didn't have any family, but of course he had a few friends, including fellow cave creepers. They didn't believe the guy would have been careless enough to fall while spelunking."

"They believed the dentist killed his partner in cold blood so he could keep the entire treasure for himself? Such behavior agrees with my experience of dentists. What do you believe?"

"I don't believe anything in particular. It could have been an accident, or it could have been murder. The cops were never able to do anything with the case."

"I don't imagine. You think this Crosby Dumpler may, with an assistant, have dropped my poor friend Kirsten out of her attic window?"

"Possibly. If he really did kill his cave-dwelling pal, he surely wouldn't hesitate to try to frighten Dr. Lund into revealing where the other two ivory ibises were. And he wouldn't think twice about breaking into a museum to steal a bird. But it's only an idea. I don't even know if Dumpler is still interested in treasure hunting. He may have gotten a belly-full already."

"How do you intend to find out?" He stopped

the car in front of a narrow two-storied house with big trees in the yard and yellow light showing from a front window.

"I don't have any ideas yet. Not the foggiest. Is this Crampton's place?"

"Yes. This is where Dr. Umbray is staying while Ollie is away on his dig. Let's hope that the lighted window is an indication of her being at home."

We exited the tin can we'd been trapped in and headed up an old brick pathway to the front porch, Eben carefully picking his way along the uneven bricks.

"You should get a cane," I suggested to Eben.

"And you should dye that graying hair of yours."

"Don't get snippy. I'm just looking out for you."

"I do wish I was as young as you."

"Me? I'm not anywhere near young."

"No one thinks he's young. Or, if he does, he doesn't like it. Ring the bell."

3

I rang the bell. In a minute, the old oak door creaked open. A pale oval face peered out at us. Even in the dim light cast by the porch lamp I could see it was a remarkable face. If I'd thought Kirsten Lund was beautiful, I'd been wrong. She looked like an old otter compared to this woman. Luminous amber eyes, with coppery highlights, a heavy fall of dark hair, also with coppery highlights, features as pure and well carved as an antique doll's. A lush figure, long limbs, with just a hint of roses high on her cheeks.

She looked at me blankly, with a hesitant smile. Then she saw Eben standing next to me, and the smile became one of the most dangerous things I'd ever seen. She might have been thirty, certainly too young to be a dowdy doctor. But maybe her perfect skin was deceiving.

"Eben," she said, her voice a breathy vibration.

"Lilith. Excuse this late intrusion of your privacy. It's important."

"Of course." She swung the door open. "Come in, both of you."

We went in. There was a little Christmas tree, a poor straggly thing, lit-up in the corner of the cluttered living room we found ourselves in. A few wrapped presents were under it. There was an old leather couch, two leather easy chairs, a hassock, a coat rack, a by-God elephant's foot umbrella stand, and a couple of pole lamps.

The room was dominated by a big stone fireplace. It had a low-burning fire in it, and it had a wide, split-log mantel whose every inch of space was taken up with a bizarre collection of knick knacks, artifacts, and junk. The walls were adorned with a series of old, dark, oil paintings, their frames ornately carved and gilded. The drapes were some kind of tapestry stuff.

The place looked like a Victorian pawn shop.

"Sit down, please," the perfect Lilith invited. "Tell me what's going on. Nothing terrible I hope?"

We sat down, each in an arm chair, and Lilith draped her lovely form on the couch, but with an eager, expectant, look on her face.

"There is no death involved," Eben assured the young woman. "It is not as bad as that, but bad enough. Let me introduce you to my friend, Axel Hatchett. He's a private investigator. Axe, this is my former colleague and friend, Lilith Umbray."

We nodded at each other.

"What's happened?" Lilith persisted.

"Our friend Kirsten has met with an accident. Some thugs — treasure hunters, apparently — accosted her at her home and dangled her from an attic window. In their enthusiasm, they dropped her into the yard and she broke her leg. She's at the hospital now."

Lilith half rose from the couch. "How could anyone do such a thing? And why?"

"These base hooligans were looking for the ivory ibis. You know the beast I'm talking about?"

"That Egyptian carving. Certainly I know it, and the silly story behind it. Did these two goons think the treasure tale was real?"

"Apparently. Kirsten had wrapped up the carving as a Christmas present for professor Snelf. It was under her Christmas tree, and likely still is. Axe and I will ascertain that later. We came to warn you, Lilith. As you no-doubt realize, there are three of these birds. The original was recently stolen from our little museum. And the other is, if I'm not mistaken, in this house."

"Oh, yes, it's on the mantel."

"I suggest you give it to us for safe keeping."

"I'm not sure of that," I interrupted. "I still think it's best if we let them steal it. Dr. Umbray will be safer that way. Just leave it on the mantel. That's my advice. By the way, could I see the thing? I'm curious."

"Of course. It's quite lovely. Kirsten is a skilled carver."

She got off the couch in one fluid movement

and walked over to the fireplace. She reached out, then stopped.

"Something wrong?" asked Eben.

"It's—it's not here. I don't understand! I know it was here. I saw it just the other day."

I went over and took a look for myself. The mantel was dusty, and there were fresh marks in the dust, but no obvious bare spot where the ibis might have been.

"Stuff has been moved around," I said. "Someone rearranged the things so the ibis wouldn't be easily missed. It's been stolen, but why would the thieves care if you knew? What's it to them?"

Lilith shook her head. "Ollie's going to be upset. I promised him I'd take care of his place while he was away. And now I've let thieves break in."

"I'm sure Ollie will be understanding," said Eben. "Well, perhaps it is better this way. The scoundrels won't be bothering you now."

"I hope that's true," I said. "But I think you need to be careful. Keep the doors locked when you're here. I suggest you call the police and report the theft. They've already talked to Dr. Lund; they'll understand the significance of the stolen statue. Actually, it might be a good idea for you to stay with someone else for a while. Can you arrange that?"

She was silent for a moment. "I guess. I hate to impose on anyone at this time of year. People all have their Christmas plans, including visiting relatives. I think I'd rather stay here. I have a gun, does that help? It's Ollie's, but he taught me how to shoot it."

I shrugged. "Having a gun's better than not having one, but I still think you'd be safer staying with someone else."

"You can stay with me," said Eben. "I don't have any family joining me this Christmas. I have a spare bedroom. Three, actually."

Lilith made a face. "I couldn't live with all those snakes, Eben. Thanks anyway."

"I can confine the snakes to their rooms."

"That's hardly fair. No, thanks, I'll be fine."

"Could I see that gun of yours?" I asked.

"Certainly. I'll go get it."

She left the room. For the first time I noticed what she was wearing. A dark red velvet robe over black and gold pajamas. She would have looked good in anything. In a minute she returned with a big revolver in her hands. She turned it over to me.

It was a Smith and Wesson Hand Ejector, a forty-four Special with a six and a half inch barrel. I swung out the cylinder and saw it was fully loaded. The gun had a beat-up look, like it'd been carried around a lot, but it looked serviceable. I handed it back to Lilith, butt first.

"That'll do the trick," I said.

"Please, come stay with me," said Eben.

She gave him a bright smile, but shook her head with finality. This was Eben's night for dealing with stubborn women.

I handed Lilith one of my business cards. "I've been hired to look into this matter. If you need anything, give me a call. Anytime, day or night. Understand?"

"Yes. Thank you. This is all so silly. How could anyone actually believe in that ridiculous ivory ibis story?"

"People believe what they want to believe." I turned to Eben. "We ought to get going if we're dropping by Dr. Lund's place tonight. I'm eager to look the place over."

Eben rose from his chair. "Yes, I suppose we ought to get going."

"I'll visit Kirsten in the hospital tomorrow," said Lilith. "She doesn't exactly like me, but I guess she'll be happy to have visitors."

"Nonsense. What do you mean she doesn't like you? Everyone likes you." said Eben.

"Kirsten's a little green-eyed," Lilith explained.

Eben raised his eyebrows. "Really? Perhaps there are things I don't know about. That's what I get for being retired."

We climbed into our coats and left. I took one more wistful glance at Lilith. "Call me if you need anything."

She nodded and gave me a smile that broke my heart.

When we were back in Eben's hot rod, I turned to him and said: "Green-eyed?"

"Well, I must say that does surprise me. Kirsten and Ollie have had an on-again, off-again, romance for years Perhaps Lilith has replaced Kirsten in Ollie's affections. I hope it doesn't cause trouble in the department. Professors can be so childish sometimes, though I hate to admit it."

"Is this Ollie guy a lady killer?"

"He has a certain rough magnetism. He treats women quite casually. You know how women are; sometimes they like being tossed to the wolves. Why is that?"

"You're asking me to explain dames? They're a mystery to me, pal."

"What about your new amata? Is she, too, an enigma?"

"Tracy? She shoots straight from the hip and she doesn't care what she hits. But, yeah, I'm sure she's got some of that enigma stuff in her. They all do."

We drove only a few blocks, and then pulled in front of another old, narrow, house. There were lights on in the lower windows.

"Looks like Minnie is home," said Eben. "I hope she's all right. The thieves entered through her bedroom window, or so the police supposed. I wonder if Minnie has any idea what's happened. Perhaps Kirsten has called her."

We walked up the broken concrete walk.

"I'm surprised more of you professors haven't broken your legs," I complained. "You ever consider maintaining your sidewalks.?"

"Wouldn't that take away some of the charm of our abodes? It's like old Europe."

"I'll settle for modern Colorado. By the way, don't you professors ever sleep? Lilith's still awake, and now Minnie."

"Minnie is a secretary, but I think she shares the night-owl attributes of the faculty. We're vampires, Axe, I thought you knew that. Actually, school's out for the holidays. We're celebrating the absence of students." Eben pushed the doorbell buzzer. I noticed cobwebs around the bulb of the porch light. In a moment the front door was jerked open and someone was shining a flashlight in our startled faces.

"Oh, Eben, it's you," said a relieved woman's voice. "Come in. Is this gentleman a police officer of some sort?"

"He's a private detective," said Eben. "Minnie, this is Axel Hatchett. Axe, my friend and former associate, Minnie."

"Come in, come in," said Minnie.

"Actually," I said, "if I could borrow your flashlight a minute, I'd like to take a look around outside first."

"Yes, of course, you're a detective." She handed me the flashlight.

"I'll accompany you," Eben told me.

"Fine, but watch your step."

I trained the flashlight beam on the ground and we made a tour of the outside of the house. The damned cops had tramped all over the place, their elephant-sized footprints destroying any kind of evidence I might have found.

"Why can't those flatfeet wear ballet slippers?" I complained to Eben.

"By all means, let's take it up with the mayor. Can you find anything at all of interest?"

"Not likely."

At the back of the house, the snow had been considerably stirred up by something other than footprints. This must have been where Lund landed. There was a big pile of snow-covered, raked-up, leaves against the foundation of the house.

"Looks like she just missed those leaves," I said. "Too bad. They would have broken her fall."

"Poor Kirsten. She had no luck at all."

"There's nothing more out here. Let's go inside."

We stomped around to the front door again, scraping our snowy shoe soles on a mat that said "Valcomen" on our way in.

"Swedish," said Eben.

"You speak it?"

"Of course not," said Eben. "I speak English and Snake."

I returned the flashlight to Minnie with my thanks. She was a little past middle age, a bit stocky, with a young girl's haircut dyed red. She had the face of a lumpy light bulb, with pink spots of rouge on her cheeks and a generous coating of red lipstick.

"Isn't it awful, Eben?" she asked.

"Appalling. Did Kirsten call you from the hospital?"

32

"Yes. I only got back a little while ago."

"I hope the villains who attacked her didn't spoil your apartment, Minnie."

"No. They didn't touch a thing, only tramped some snow on my carpet. Hot chocolate?"

"Some other time," I said. "Thanks."

"None for me. Thank you, Minnie."

"How do we get upstairs?" I asked.

"I think the door is unlocked." Minnie gestured toward a door parallel to her own apartment door. I tried the knob. It turned.

We climbed some steep carpeted steps and came to a landing and another door. This one opened too. We went in and turned on some lights. The place was a wreck. We went through every inch of it.

The second story contained the living room, dining room, bedroom, guest room, kitchen and bathroom. Furniture was pulled away from the walls. Sofa and chair cushions littered the floor. In the bedrooms, drawers had been pulled from dressers and bureaus and the mattresses had been wrenched from the beds. Even the refrigerator had been gone through.

The third floor, the attic, was just one big room. There was a desk and bookcases on one side. The books had been pulled from the shelves. The desk drawers were lying on the floor. Even the fake Persian carpet had been pulled up. The rest of the attic consisted of a big workshop with a workbench scattered with carving tools and wood shavings. There were shelves against the walls that had recently held quite a collection of wood, ivory and bone carvings, mostly figures of animals or people. They were beautiful, but now they were knocked all over the floor. Some of the carvings were quite delicate in appearance. The doctor, as a wood carver, knew her stuff.

I looked out the window that Lund must have been dangled out of. I paid special attention to the paint on the window sill, where Lund must have straddled before she was dropped. The paint was old and chipped in spots, but none of the chips looked new.

"You see anything wrong about this place?" I asked Eben.

"What? Everything's wrong. It looks like it was hit by a large and angry cyclone."

"Sure. Anything else?"

"Why, no. You're the detective. What do you see that's wrong?"

"Nothing's broken. All these fragile carvings are still intact. Not so much as a light bulb is broken in this place. For a couple of hasty thieves, these guys were strangely protective of Lund's possessions."

Eben started turning red, and his mouth grew hard. "What are you suggesting, Axe?"

"Nothing. Not a damned thing."

"Yes you are. Spill it."

"'Spill it'? You trying to talk like a gumshoe? I'm not suggesting anything. I'm just bothered a little, that's all."

"You can't fool me. I know what you're think-ing. You think — for whatever impossible reason — that Kirsten, the esteemed Dr. Lund, rifled her own apartment to make it look like a break-in. Why would she do such a thing? And then what? She threw herself out of the window and broke her own leg? I—"

"Take it easy, Eben, I'm warning you. If you want to help me with this investigation, you need to keep an open mind. I'm trying to."

"Yes, but to insult my revered colleague, and in such a preposterous manner — "

"Button your lip, Eben. If you can't help me, I can go it alone. Or we can just forget the whole thing."

He sputtered and stamped his foot. Then he be-gan laughing, a merry sound.

"There's the old Eben," I said. I went over and patted his arm. "It's been a long night for you, old friend. Take it easy. I'm just trying to do my job."

"You just called me old, twice, in only two sen-tences. And you think I need a cane. I ought to mop up the floor with you, you impudent whelp."

He started laughing again. "I didn't mean to get up on my hind legs, Axe, I really didn't. But I must say you did offend me. For the future I shall contrive to be as cold and steely a blood hound as yourself. And you're right, it is odd that nothing in the apartment is broken. We must find the ex-planation."

"I don't think there's much more for us to do here. We should be going. We both could use some sleep."

"Could we clean up a little first? I hate to think of Kirsten coming home to this place the way it is."

"Sure, that's a swell idea."

We spent about half an hour putting the carvings back on the shelves, the books in their bookcases, all the drawers back where they belonged, and the mattresses back on the beds. The apartment looked a lot better than it had when we'd entered.

Before we left, we checked out the Christmas tree. Of all the things in the apartment, the tree was the only thing that had gone untouched. I found a clumsily-wrapped present with 'To Ray' on the tag and tore it open. There was a box under the wrapping, and in the box was an ivory ibis. It was beautifully carved — the figure of a standing man with the head of a long-beaked bird. It was decorated with black and gold paint. On the bottom was a label that said: 'Treasure Map Inside.' A joke.

"Do you want to hang onto this, or should I?" I asked Eben.

"Whatever you think is best."

"I'll keep it then. I'll put it in a safe place."

"Do so. And be careful."

"I'm always careful. There's only one Axel Hatchet, and I don't want the number reduced."

"What's your middle name, by the way?"

"Burton."

"Axel Burton Hatchett. It has a sort of poetry, don't you think?"

"Sure, just like its owner."

We went downstairs, and Minnie waylaid us.

"Did you discover anything?" she eagerly asked us.

"We'll see," Eben told her. "The detective business is a complicated one, and a secretive one, as well. Good night, dear Minnie."

We got back into Eben's roller-skate, and he drove me back to the hospital to pick up my car.

"Lilith. That's an interesting name," I mentioned to Eben. "It's kind of mythological, isn't it? Wasn't Lilith Adam's second wife, after Eve dumped him? Isn't that the story?"

"Why, Axe, you really did finish elementary school. I thought you were just bragging. The name Lilith has quite a history. But, yes, according to some tales she was the wife of Adam. But she was his first wife. She left him."

"Probably had something going on with a guy God didn't know about."

"Perhaps. Why do you bring up the subject?"

"Just talking. Just passing the time," I told him.

"I see."

"When is Ollie Crampton coming back to town?"

"I don't know. I don't expect him back until after New Year's."

"I wish he'd get back sooner."

"You could call him."

"Yeah? Who's going to pay for the long distance bill?"

"I will, Axe, if you really want to talk to him. I think there's a ranch near his dig where he can be reached. That's what Kirsten told me."

"No, I don't need to call him. Not yet, anyway."

"Tell me what you're thinking."

"I'm not much for sharing, Eben. Tomorrow I need to look up that old treasure hunting client of mine. I hope he's in town. Christmas screws up everything."

"That's the spirit."

"Say, that reminds me. If a young buck like you was going to pick up a Christmas gift for a special girl, what would it be?"

"A snake?"

"You're still thinking of Eve. No, something a little more conventional."

"A new auto."

"Something cheaper. Besides, she has a car."

"Are you asking me to pick out a gift for your intended?"

"I'm only fishing for suggestions, Eben."

"Jewelry's always nice."

"She's not big on jewelry. I already gave her a ring."

"A fur coat?"

"She wouldn't wear it. She'd be afraid of ruining it."

"Perhaps, but gifts need not always be practical. She might appreciate the gesture."

"I thought of a fruitcake."

"Think again. Fruitcakes are for maiden aunts. I'm afraid you're on your own. You are the one who knows the young lady."

"Maybe a pony. Hell, I wish I could think of something. She'll probably get me something swell. I don't want to look like a sap. I want to get her a good present. She's a special kid."

"You're running out of time."

"Don't remind me. How about a nice fluffy kitten?"

"Good luck finding one. Does your one-and-only like cats?"

"Damned if I know. But I do know where I can get one. A neighbor of mine has a cat that had kittens a few weeks ago. It's a pretty homely cat, kind of looks like a horned toad. But the kittens look OK. One of them's pretty ornery and mean looking. Reminds me of Tracy."

"Use your own judgment."

"I wish I didn't have to."

"Perhaps two kittens. They can keep each other company."

"Sure. Maybe I'll spring for the whole litter."

4

When we reached the hospital, I guided Eben over to where my ride was parked. The night was still clear. When I got out of the Volkswagen, the cold air hit me like a slap. I leaned in through the open passenger door to tell my friend goodnight. The dome light showed me his face. He looked older than I'd ever seen him.

"It's going to be OK, Eben. I'll find whoever dropped your pal out the window. Dr. Lund's safe enough in the hospital. Go home and get some sleep."

He looked at me and tried on a wan smile. "Keep me apprised of matters. Thank you for your help, and for your assurances that Kirsten will be all right. I'm glad I have a detective for a friend."

"You've got bad taste.. Let me know if anything comes up."

"Listen, when you visit your murdering treasure hunter, if you do, let me know."

"OK. Why?'

"I wouldn't mind being in on the kill, as they say."

"You want to go with me to talk to the guy?"

"How else am I going to learn to be a crack detective? I need to study your methods."

"I might not want you around. I mean, I'm used to doing things by myself, and whatever talk I have with Dumpler might require a certain amount of crafty delicacy."

"I can be delicate." He looked almost offended.

"Yeah. Well, we'll see. I'll call you later."

"Thank you for taking on the case. Do we need to discuss the contract?"

"No. I won't cheat you. And if you don't want to pay me, don't."

"Of course I'll pay you. Any amount you say."

"Really? Wow! Looks like I'll be buying Tracy jewelry and a fur coat. Just kidding."

I slammed the German sauerkraut can's door and walked to my Nash. I started it, put it in gear, and drove home. I was just getting ready to climb into bed when the damned phone rang. I figured it might be Eben.

"Hello?"

"Where you been?"

Tracy. My girl.

"I've been sleeping."

"Not unless you can sleep through a hundred phone rings. I've been trying to call you since midnight."

"I was on the phone at midnight."

"I know. I got a busy signal. Who were you talking to so late? Is she cute? Does she have masses of flowing hair and a killer figure?"

"I was talking to a man, and he doesn't have flowing masses of hair. Eben Mulford. I've told you about him. I'm working on a case. Why have you been calling me? Are you all right?"

"I'm fine, but I'm a little lonely. I wanted to hear your scratchy voice."

"Oh, OK. I've been thinking of you, too, potato cookie."

I told her as much as I knew about Dr. Lund's getting dumped out a window.

"What do you think about the case?" she asked.

"I think it stinks like a month-old mackerel. But I don't have any kind of handle on it yet. Any ideas?"

"I think you need to talk to that guy you just mentioned. What's his name? The treasure hunter."

"Dumpler. Crosby Dumpler."

"He sounds like your best bet, maybe."

"Maybe is right. I don't know. I'll try looking him up tomorrow."

"You're going to go see him? You aren't going to call?"

"You know how I work. I like to see people when I talk to them. I just hope he's in town."

"Can I go with you?"

"To see Dumpler? Hell, no. Why would you want to?"

"You know why. You said that after we're married I might be able to help you with your investigating. This will give me practice."

"No. It's going to be a delicate interview, if it comes off at all."

"Can you honestly say you know anyone with more delicacy than me?"

"Well, maybe Attila the Hun, but I don't really know him. Stay out of this one, Tracy. Eben's already asked to go along, and I certainly don't need two junior detectives with me."

"If Eben's going, then you have to take me too. It's only fair."

"The world isn't fair, sweet meat."

"Maybe not, but you are. Let me go see Dumpler with you. I won't get in the way, I'll be helpful. And I really do want to learn how to help you. If Eben's going then I should be able to go, too."

"Did I say you couldn't come with me to talk to Dumpler?"

"Yes. That was you who said that."

"Perhaps I was too hasty. Tell you what, if I really do take Eben with me, then you can come along too."

"That's better."

"Listen, I'll drop by Rocko's tomorrow. Are you working?"

"Always. You can meet the new waitress."

"You're kidding! Cookie hired a new girl?"

"My replacement. He says once I'm married I won't be reliable. I'll have to start looking for a new job."

"We'll find you something a whole lot better for you than Rocko's Kitchen."

"I hope so. In the meantime, I've got to train this new kid. She's pretty, and sweet, and polite."

"And she's supposed to be your replacement? Why didn't he hire someone more like you?"

"There's nobody like me, cherry lips, you know that."

"Sure. What's her name?"

Prissy May."

"You're joking."

"I'm not. And—you know what?—she fits her name."

"I'm sorry for her. Listen, I've got to get some shut-eye. You too."

"Sleep well my lovely crumb cake."

"See you later, my little soft pretzel."

I went to bed and dreamed that zebras were chasing me down a dark alley. I woke up before they caught me.

I was finishing the second half of a full pot of coffee when the phone rang. It was Eben.

"Axe? Eben. Kirsten spent a bad night, but she had less pain this morning. She's very restless. She's talking of renting a wheel chair and leaving the hospital."

"She needs to stay where she is. She's safe in the hospital. Besides, they wouldn't really let her go, would they?"

"I doubt it, but she might sneak out. I'm trying

to talk some sense into her."

"Good. Keep talking to her."

"Have you spoken to the dentist yet?"

"No, I just got up. I'll call him at his office."

"And if you meet him somewhere, you'll give me a call first?"

"Are you sure you want to meet him, Eben?"

"I look forward to it."

"All right. I'll call you."

I'd left the ibis in its box on my nightstand. I needed a place to hide it. I couldn't find one. Then I had an idea. I looked out my kitchen window to see if my neighbor, Blythe Bliss, had gone to work yet. Her Pontiac was still parked behind her little log cabin cottage. Blythe and I live in part of a row of old motel cottages that are now year-around rentals. She's a cop, but an all right dame despite that. The ibis should be safe in a cop's house. I grabbed the bird and headed next door. When I knocked she opened the door right away.

"My hair's still wet," she greeted me. "Here to see the kittens again? You better pick one soon. I've got other interested buyers. Kittens are hard to come by this time of year. How that tabby of mine linked up with that ugly tom I'll never figure out. Come on in."

Blythe is from west Texas and has all the unnecessary friendliness of that tribe. I followed her into the living room where a big striped cat was fussily grooming five kittens.

"I've got a favor to ask you," I said. "A client of

mine needs to hide a package, something they don't want anyone else to get ahold of. It's small." I showed her the box. "I don't suppose you could stick it under your bed, or in the icebox, or under the kittens, or someplace, just for a few days?"

"I might could do that. What is it?"

"A bird. Here, I'll show you." I took the figure out of its box and Blythe ooed and ahed over it.

"What kind of a bird is that? I never saw one like it in Texas."

"I would hope not. Do you have a lot of birds with men's bodies in Texas?'

"Not that I recall."

"It's an Egyptian ibis. It represents the god Thoth, I believe."

"Well, aren't we educated! Sure, I'll hide him for you. You decided which kitten you want yet?"

"I'm thinking of getting a pair. Would that be all right?"

"Well, like I said, I've got folks interested. But, sure, you can buy two. The money's going to the police relief program you know."

"An excellent cause. Let me take another look at these little guys." I walked over to the box where the mama cat and her brood were. Mama gave me an icy glare, but I ignored her. I picked up the little orangey ornery one and it began mewing. "Which are the girls and which are the boys?" I asked.

"I thought you were a man of the world. Check them out for yourself."

I discovered the ornery one was a boy.

"Is it better to have two girls, two boys, or a mix?" I asked.

"Well, from what I know from cats, most likely two toms would get along best. And then you wouldn't have to worry about kittens in the future."

"True." I found another boy. He was a kind of yellowish-cream color. I took a good look at the two. I wouldn't say either one of them were exactly cute. They had fierce faces and there fur grew out in uneven tufts. "You'll keep these guys a few days longer for me, if I agree to buy them?"

"Sure. Be happy too. Are those the two you want? They're the ugliest."

"Think so? Well, at least they match."

"You're right about that."

"Do I pay you now?"

"No. I trust you."

"Thanks. Then I'll take these two."

"Congratulations, Daddy."

"Thanks. I feel proud. But I don't mean to delay you. I know you've got to get to work."

"Oh, yeah, that again. Must be nice to be a detective and keep your own hours."

"You wouldn't like my hours, believe me."

I said good-bye and went back to my place. I called Tracy to tell her I was on my way.

"Prissy May is dying to meet you," Tracy told me.

"Yeah? Tell her I'm just dying to meet her, too."

I fired up the red Nash and headed for Rocko's .

My stomach grumbled all the way, but not from hunger. Fear. Rocko's food would frighten any self-respecting belly. While I drove I thought about the ivory ibis and everything I'd learned about Kirsten Lund's attack. I didn't know much. I decided to call Crosby Dumpler as soon as I'd had my breakfast — or late lunch, as it was turning out — and see if I could finagle a meeting with him. He was a guy who liked to chew the fat, so I figured he might be willing to see me.

I pulled up in front of Rocko's Kitchen and went inside. Tracy greeted me with a chaste kiss on the cheek, then introduced me to Prissy May. She was a swell girl, as fresh and sweet as a dewy daisy. When I walked in, she was smiling lovingly at a male customer, a trucker by his looks, who was loudly complaining about the rubbery nature of his fried eggs.

"We'll be happy to fry another couple of eggs for you, sir," Prissy May told him. "On the house, of course."

Tracy turned as red as my Nash and bore down on the trucker.

"Eat those eggs — they're perfectly cooked," she told him. "If you had decent teeth you wouldn't have any trouble chewing them. Rubbery!"

The trucker stood up, still masticating a mouthful of egg. "You can't talk to me like that," he yelled. "What kind of place is this, anyhow?"

"It's a wholesome eatery," said Tracy. "Now finish your breakfast and get out. And don't forget to pay."

The poor guy hurried through the rest of his meal and threw some change on the counter. "Last time I'm coming into this greasy dive."

"None of us are going to miss you," said Tracy.

"I will," said Prissy May, smiling.

The trucker banged the door on leaving and Tracy turned her wrath on Prissy May.

"Prissy, I'm tired of having to tell you this five times a day. In Rocko's, the customer is always wrong. That's simple enough, isn't it? And quit smiling so much."

"Yes, Tracy," the girl said, smiling so broadly that dimples appeared in her apple cheeks. "But the eggs really were kind of rubbery."

"That makes them easier to digest. Look, Cookie learned to sling hash when he was in the Navy. He doesn't do a very good job of it. If you keep trying to satisfy his customers, he's going to end up firing you. I'm trying to look out for you, OK? You stay here and watch the counter while I go out front a minute and talk to my fiancée."

"Yes, Tracy."

5

When we were out on the sidewalk, with the door closed behind us, Tracy fumed silently for a minute.

"She's impossible," she told me. "She's perfect. Half our customers are sweet on her. They sit around slurping the same cup of five-cent coffee for half an hour, just so they can gawp at her. She's polite. She scrubs the counter so clean you can see all the cracks and chips in it. The dirt usually hides that stuff. She never gets mad at anybody, and she's all the time trying to satisfy the customers, the chumps. She's costing us money. I don't know what Cookie was thinking when he hired her."

"Take it easy. Maybe she'll get worse. Working at Rocko's won't improve her temperament any. Who knows? In time she might become as sour as you. Come on, sweet potato, quit riding the kid so hard. Why don't you get mad at Cookie instead?"

"I don't dare. He'd fire me."

"He's going to fire you pretty soon anyhow. You looking for another job yet?"

"Of course I am. Every chance I get I'm looking for a new job."

"I'm sure you'll find one soon. I'll keep my eyes and ears open for you."

She smiled suddenly and looked almost happy. "You talk to your treasure hunter murderer yet?"

"I'll call him after I've eaten. Say, do you think Prissy May could serve my breakfast to me?"

Tracy gave me the kind of look a skunk would give a perfume bottle.

"Just kidding," I said.

"I can hardly wait to meet the treasure hunter. What is he, a dentist?"

"That's right."

"I got a wisdom tooth that's bothering me."

"Is that why you're in such a bad mood? I'm sure he'll be happy to take a look at it, and he won't charge you more than an arm and a leg. Listen, Tracy, I don't think it's a great idea for you to go with me to talk to Dumpler. I need to handle this alone."

"Alone? Does that mean Eben's not going with you?"

"Well, I haven't told him yet, but, yeah, I don't want him going with me either."

"You just want all the credit, don't you? Big shot detective."

"There's no talking to you today — you're too upset about Prissy May. Let's go back inside, I'm hungry."

"Wait! I just want to help you, OK? We're going to be getting married soon. I can be your girl Friday, but I want to be more than a secretary. I want to help you with your investigations. Now's a great time to start."

"I don't know. You're certainly smart enough to help me out. I wish you'd start wearing your glasses, though. You squint like a hen laying a three-cornered egg. Gumshoes need to be able to see. Come on, let's go back inside."

I ordered my usual: fried eggs, bacon, toast, coffee. Everything was awful. Tracy let the new girl serve me. She was sweet and attentive. I sincerely hoped Cookie didn't ruin her.

"How are those eggs, Axe? Too rubbery?" Tracy challenged me.

"I like them that way. Gives me a chance to exercise my jaw muscles. A man's got to keep in shape you know." I finished my meal, paid for it, and slid a quarter tip across the counter to Prissy May. I couldn't resist.

"Thank you, Mr. Hatchett. I hope you'll come back soon. I think Tracy's so lucky to have a real detective for a future husband."

"He gets shot at too much," said Tracy. "And he works round-the-clock sometimes. Still, you're right, it is kind of exciting. He just needs to learn to stay away from the slinky dames."

"Half my clients are slinky dames," I said.

"My point exactly. Can I get you some apple

pie for dessert?"

"Cookie actually baked a pie?" I was surprised. "What's in it? Rotten apples and stale lard?"

"Naw, he didn't bake it himself. There's a bakery down the street that he's started buying pastries from. Cookie's trying to branch out a little."

"Maybe he could hire a cook, too."

"Fat chance. He thinks he's a master chef."

"Say, let me borrow your phone," I said.

"Help yourself. It's on the wall where it always is."

I went around the back of the counter and took the receiver off the hook. I had already looked up Dumpler's number before I left home. I dialed it.

"Dumpler's Nearly Painless Dentistry. May I help you?"

"Yeah. Can I speak with Dr. Dumpler?"

"He's with a patient. May I take a message, or schedule an appointment?"

"This is Axe Hatchett. Tell him I want to talk to him about a treasure map."

"I'll give him the message. What's the call-back number, please?"

I gave the spritely-voiced receptionist Rocko's number, then I killed time talking to Tracy and trying to eat a donut that must have been November's. In a few minutes, the phone rang. Prissy May answered it, and then passed the receiver to me.

"It's for you. Mr. Hatchet," she said, brightly. Her eyes shown like freshly-mined sapphires.

"This is Hatchett. Yeah, I wanted to talk to you about a treasure map mystery I'm working on."

"I was just finishing up a root canal."

"Give your patient my condolences. Listen, I'm going to be out in your area in a little bit. Mind if I stop by and talk with you for a couple of minutes?"

"Well, can't we handle this over the phone? I've got a pretty tight schedule today."

"I don't trust phones. You never know who's listening in. When is your last appointment?"

"I should be finished up by half past three."

"Is it OK if I drop by then? I need your expertise."

"I guess."

I glanced over at Tracy. Her arms were crossed over her cushiony bosom and her basilisk's glare was attempting to turn me to stone.

"Listen, I'm on a case right now, concerning this treasure map. I'll have a couple of operatives with me, do you mind? They're fans of yours, actually. I told them all about your finding that gold in the Foggy Tops."

I heard him sigh. "All right, but I can't spare you much of my time."

"Swell. We'll see you at four. Thanks, Doc." I hung up. Tracy was smiling at me now.

"This will be so much fun," she said.

I grumbled something I hoped she didn't hear and used the phone again to call Eben.

"The game's afoot," I told him. "Can you meet

me at Dumpler's Nearly Painless Dentistry at four?"

"I don't know where it is, but I'll find out. I'll see you then."

"Sure. Bring your Captain Midnight Decoder Ring."

I hung out at Rocko's, waiting for the clock hands to move some more while Tracy gave Prissy May instructions on how to behave while she was gone.

"Don't give out anything for free. Don't offer to remake an order. Don't make a customer so comfortable that he'll want to hang around. Don't be nice, and don't smile."

"Yes, Tracy." Her smile was like spring sunshine.

It was almost four when Tracy and I piled into the Nash and headed for the land of painless dentistry.

"I can't wait to meet this guy," Tracy told me, once we were on our way. She was in a great mood now. "Does he look like a murderer?"

"He looks like a dentist."

"So he looks like a murderer."

"Let me do the talking when we get there, OK? I've got to be careful how I question this guy. I don't want him to clam up."

"I won't say a word."

"Promise."

"No, I can't do that. Something might come up. I might need to say something."

"You can wish Dr. Dumpler a Merry Christmas. How's that?"

"We'll see."

The dental office was in a newer, pricier, part of town than my usual haunts. It was located in a one story, stand-alone, building of glass and concrete, in the middle of a fair piece of land planted with young pine trees. When we pulled into the spacious parking lot, I didn't see Eben's little German kiddy car. I hoped he wouldn't be late. But he wasn't. It was only three-fifty when his car pulled up next to us. We all got out and I introduced Tracy and Eben.

"So this is the soon-to-be Mrs. Hatchett. Charming, my dear, you're absolutely charming."

I always thought Tracy was above cheap flattery, but she colored up like a school girl.

""You're the famous snake professor Axe has told me about. How many snakes do you own?"

"An even dozen."

"Why not make it a baker's dozen?"

"I intend to. Are you a snake fancier?"

"I'm partial to them, yes. Did you know Axe is scared of snakes?"

"I am not," I protested. "I just don't like the slimy, wiggly, things around me, that's all. I'm not scared of anything, except maybe you. Let's get inside. It's cold out here."

It was cold. The sky had become overcast and it felt like snow. We went inside. The waiting room was a swell place, all bright tile floor, white walls, and blond Danish modern furniture. A young la-dy—also blonde, possibly Danish — dressed in-a nurses' uniform, sat behind a glassed-in counter and greeted us brightly. I suspect she'd been hired mostly for her picturesque qualities.

"We're here to see Dr. Dumpler," I informed her. "He's expecting us. I'm Axe Hatchett."

"Yes, Mr. Hatchett, I'll tell Doctor you're here." She left her post and returned a moment later and led us back to a sparkling room with a kitchen ta-ble and chairs, and its own fridge and sink. Dumpler was sitting at the table, unwrapping a waxed-paper-covered sandwich. It looked like deviled ham. He stood up to shake hands all around.

"Pardon me," he said. "I'm having a late lunch. It's been a busy day and this is the first moment I've had for a break."

"Dr. Dumpler, these are my associates, Tracy Clover and Dr. Eben Mulford."

"Oh, a doctor? Not a dentist, are you?"

"No, too squeamish," said Eben. "I'm a retired professor of British Literature."

"I see. I know a couple of professors from the college."

"Do you know a Dr. Lund, or Dr. Crampton?" I asked.

"Ollie and I have crossed paths. Archeologist, isn't he? He hunts artifacts up in the Foggy Tops. I do a bit of gold hunting there."

"Some pretty successful hunting," I said.

"How exciting," said Tracy. I thought she was going to ask for his autograph.

"I understand that most of the gold mines in the Foggy Tops are played out," said Eben. "But I imagine there's still quite a bit of treasure tucked away in those hills."

"Enough to make us all quite wealthy," said Dumpler. He was wearing a starched lab coat with a bit of someone's blood on one sleeve. "What can I do for you?"

"Well," I said, "I want to talk to you about a treasure map I've heard tell of. I'm in the middle of a case. My client was attacked by thieves trying to steal the map. She was dropped from a window and broke her leg."

"How terrible! Someone did this to her?"

"Two guys. Listen, have you ever heard of the ivory ibis treasure?"

He laughed, showing big horse teeth. "A legend. I've heard the story. Nonsense, nothing but nonsense."

"From what I've heard, I agree with you," I said. "But someone's taking the story seriously. I don't suppose you have any interest in Egyptian artifacts?"

"Not really. I'm a local boy. Most of my interest is in the Foggy Tops. Even if I believed in the ivory ibis legend, I wouldn't be keen to pursue it. I couldn't justify leaving my practice long enough to make a trip to Egypt. Besides, I'm sure those artifacts are protected by law by now."

"And you wouldn't want to do anything illegal. But not all treasure hunters are as honest as you."

"Unfortunately, no."

"Is it true," asked Tracy, "that your partner got killed helping you find that collection of gold religious statues?"

Dumpler's face clouded. He bit into his sandwich and ruminated on it.

"Yes, my partner fell to his death. It was tragic, tragic."

"But it meant more gold for you, right?" Tracy asked.

I tried to kick her under the table where we were all sitting.

Dumpler finished chewing and cleared his throat.

"My personal gain in no way diminished my sadness over my partner's untimely death."

"How much were those gold figures worth?" asked Eben, "If you don't mind sharing that information."

"Nowhere near what some people think. I made enough to finance my search, but not a great deal more."

"But now you're searching for more treasure?" asked Eben.

"Yes. It gets in one's blood. You should try it yourself sometime."

"Well," said Eben, "excuse me if I don't volunteer to be your partner."

This time I tried kicking Eben under the table.

"I'm afraid I can't help you any," Dumpler told me, pointedly ignoring my clumsy operatives. "I'm just not interested in Egyptian fairytales."

"But you must know other treasure hunters. Do you know of any who might lick their chops over the ivory ibis?" I asked.

"No. I should think someone at the college is responsible for the attack on your client. Irresponsible students, perhaps. Or some demented professor."

"There are no demented educators at Flinders College, sir," said Eben, with dignity. "Eccentric, maybe, but not demented."

"I'm happy to hear it," said the dentist. "And now, if you'll excuse me, I really must get going. My wife's expecting me."

"Do you have time to look at my swollen wisdom tooth?" asked Tracy.

"I'm afraid not. But there are many other dentists in Quartz Quarry."

"OK. You probably charge too much anyway," said Tracy.

"I can't abide visiting the dentist," volunteered Eben. "It seems a strangely medieval branch of medicine."

I stood up. "Sorry to take up so much of your time, Dr. Dumpler," I said. "I guess we'll be going. Thanks for your help."

"Yes, certainly. Good luck with your little mystery."

I shooed my associates out of the building.

When we reached the parking lot, I told them: "You guys are both fired."

"What about severance pay?" asked Tracy.

"None for you, sister. What's wrong with the two of you, anyway? You treated him like a criminal. Some help you were."

"He is a criminal," said Tracy. "He murdered his partner. Did you notice how close together his eyes were?"

"And his hands were fidgety," observed Eben. "He kept clenching and unclenching them. It was as if he wanted to strangle someone."

"Imagine that," I said. "From now on, this case is mine and mine alone. You two need to get packed off to a nice finishing school. And folks call me rough around the edges!"

"It's not just the edges," said Tracy.

Eben shivered. "I've never been in the presence of a crazed murderer before."

"We don't know if Dumpler's a murderer. The cops never tagged him for it. Besides, don't be so sure you haven't looked a killer in the eye. You may have worked with one, or had one for a neighbor, or bought snake food from one. In fact, they seldom look like what they are. Some of them look like Grandma Moses."

"Grandma Moses with shifty eyes and a sneer," said Tracy.

"Listen, let's get going. I've got work to do."

"What's your next step?" asked Eben.

"I'm not sure. I'm thinking about it."

"Aren't you going to keep investigating Dumpler?" asked Tracy. "Don't you think he's guilty?"

"You heard him, he has no interest in that silly ibis story."

"That's what he wanted us to believe," said Eben. "He seemed very much in a hurry to pooh-pooh the treasure story."

"Maybe," I said, "but I believed him when he told us he couldn't conveniently make a trip to Egypt."

"He could get someone else to go," said Tracy. "Maybe the goons who broke Dr. Lund's leg. Does he have kids?"

"He's got a nephew, I think," I said. "Come to think of it, Dumpler might have mentioned to me once that his nephew goes to Flinders college."

"There, you see?" said Eben. "I certainly would not make the assumption that the dentist is not somehow involved in all this."

"I hate to admit it," I said, "but you two junior-detectives might be right. I think I'll try to track down Dumpler's nephew."

"You see, you needed us after all," said Tracy. "I like this detective business. Can I borrow one of your guns, Axe?"

"No, but I'll let you hold my fedora if you're a good girl. Come on; let's clear out of this place."

We headed for our cars.

6

I made sure to open the car door for Tracy. She's trying to turn me into a gentleman. Eben stepped over to us before we could get into the Nash.

"It occurred to me that you might want to meet some of my fellow professors," he told me, "in case they might be involved with Kirsten's—accident."

"I thought you told Dumpler none of your professors were demented?"

"I was merely defending my tribe from the aspersions cast by a dentist, of all people. Brilliant scholars and teachers are sometimes—shall we say—unstable. The English department Christmas party is tonight, at Dean Gallcarver's home. As an emeritus, I've been invited. We're allowed to bring a guest. Axe, I'm inviting you."

"Do I have to wear a corduroy jacket with patches on the elbows?"

"Wear what you wish, within reason. The party

starts at seven. Meet me at my place and we can walk over. Dean Gallcarver's house is only two blocks from my own. What do you say?"

"Sounds like a good idea. I'll be at your house a little before seven. Say, is Minnie working today?"

"We've only a skeleton crew at the college this time of year. As Secretary, Minnie might be in her office, but she might also be home."

"I'll track her down. I've got a few questions for her."

"Can I come with you?" asked Tracy.

"No. I want you to go back to Rocko's and get a lesson in manners from Prissy May." I turned to Eben. "I'll keep in touch. If you need to tell me something, call my office number, or try me at home. Or call Rocko's and leave a message."

"Certainly. Don't forget to meet me at my place so we can go to the party."

"I won't forget. What do you think I am, an absent minded professor?"

"Our minds are never absent, merely over active. Good bye, Axe. Good bye, Tracy, it's been a pleasure."

"Nice to meet you, Eben. I hope that murdering dentist doesn't give you nightmares."

"Eben has his snakes sing lullabies to him," I said.

"If only they could sing," said Eben, wistfully. "What sweet music that would be."

"If you say so. Come on, Tracy, I'll take you back to Rocko's"

We got into our respective cars and vacated the land of painless dentistry.

"My wisdom tooth really is bothering me," Tracy said as we motored back to the greasy dive she worked at.

"I'll give you the number of my dentist. He's cheap."

"Is he painless?"

"Only when he's asleep. You get what you pay for. Besides, after what you did to me in that interview with Dumpler, you deserve a little pain."

"What'd I say?"

"You implied he was a murderer."

"That's what he is. Did you see his smile? Like a rabid wolverine's."

"Skip it. See if you can get a dental appointment tomorrow. I don't want your tooth spoiling our Christmas."

"That'd be awful. No elk roast. No mashed potatoes and gravy. No chocolate pie."

"Listen, are you sure we have to go to your folks for Christmas dinner? Couldn't the two of us go out to a nice restaurant?"

"No. You need to get to know my parents. You're going to be part of the family soon."

"Yeah, but I'm not marrying your folks."

"The dinner will be fine. You'll see. Mom's great, and Pop's not bad if you get enough eggnog down him. You'll have fun. Bing Crosby records, Mom's great cooking, presents under the tree. I can hardly wait."

"That makes one of us. I wish I didn't have a case right now. I could use the time looking for a nice little apartment for the two of us for when we get married."

"You sure New Years is a good time for a wedding?"

"I thought you were in a hurry? New Year's Day is a great day to get married. New beginnings and all that."

"Sure, you're right. Who's this Minnie you're going to see? A secretary? Is she a looker?"

"No. just a nice middle-aged lady. Really."

"What about those two professor broads you told me about? Lund and Umbrage?"

"Umbray. What about them?"

"Nice middle-aged ladies?"

"Lookers, especially Lilith Umbray. An angel fresh from the beauty parlor."

"Don't forget who you're engaged to."

"How could I? Besides, you don't think a divine number like Lilith would fall for a dog-faced mug like me, do you?"

"I fell for you."

"True. And, according to Eben, you're charming."

"He's a very astute man. Do his snakes have names?"

"Yes, and probably their own wardrobes. Don't mention snakes, OK?"

"I thought you said you weren't scared of them?"

"I don't like going around mentioning my Achilles' heel. But, yeah, the slithery things give me the creeps. Here we are back at the famous Rocko's Kitchen. Give Prissy May my best."

"I'll give her a slap on the ear if she's been giving food away to griping customers. Give me a call later. And stay away from that Lilith movie star."

"If my job depends on it, I'll have to talk to her. She's quite the little siren, but you've got nothing to worry about, my little pickled herring."

"What do you want for Christmas?"

"You mean you haven't bought me anything yet?"

"I can't think what to get you."

"How about a mustache cup?"

"That might just be what you'll get. I'll check the antique shops."

"Do that." We shared a brief, steamy, kiss and I headed back toward the college.

Secretaries are founts of gossip and other information. I had high hopes Minnie might put me on the trail of the treasure hunters. She no doubt saw plenty of students and teachers. And janitors and administrators, for that matter. And she seemed like the kind of person who liked to talk, and who liked sticking her pink nose into the whole world's business.

I decided to try her at home first. It'd been dark when I'd seen Kirsten and Minnie's shared house, and Eben had been driving, but I found the place again all right. There was an old Dodge parked at the curb, and I remembered seeing it there last night. I hoped it belonged to Minnie.

I picked my way up the now ice-covered walk and rang the bell. In a couple of minutes, Minnie opened up and let me in.

"Mr. Handaxe, isn't it?"

"Hatchett. Call me Axe."

She showed me into a living room that was fairly cluttered. There were dirty breakfast dishes on an armchair, a pile of mail on another, and some clothes—including a bra and girdle — on the carpeted floor.

"Excuse the mess," she apologized, clearing a space for me on the couch, "I wasn't expecting visitors."

"Don't worry about me. You should see my place. Listen, I was wondering if I could talk to you about this whole ivory ibis business. I assume Dr. Lund has told you about what happened."

Her face lit up like I'd just given her the best Christmas present ever.

"She told me all about it and it's awful. Who would do such a thing?"

"I was hoping you could give me some ideas. I'm not asking you to finger anybody. Only tell me if you're suspicious of someone in particular. Professors, students, vagrants, anybody."

"Vagrants! Fortunately, we don't have any of those. As for the students, well, any number of them could have pushed Dr. Lund out the window. They get worse each year, I swear."

"Yeah, they're a bad lot. Any young scholars in particular you have your eye on?"

"The Fitzmont twins. They'd be capable of anything. They are the wildest girls you could imagine. They play hockey. If a girl in my day had played hockey they would have suspected her of being a boy."

"You can't trust hockey players. Or soccer players either. Some sports just call for bad blood. Are these Fitzmont monsters still on campus?"

"Well, no. They've gone home for the holidays, like so many of the other students. The campus is like a ghost town this time of year. Not that I mind."

"So the twins are miles and miles away from here?"

"Toledo, I believe."

"Girl hockey players from Toledo. What'll they think of next?"

"So, I guess it couldn't have been them. Of course, we have a lot of students who could use more spending money, the way they let it run through their fingers like water. But I can't think of anyone specifically. I don't want to judge."

"Of course not. What about the faculty? Any treasure hunters among them? Or just guys or gals who are nuts?"

"Nuts. That makes me think of Dr. Snelf. Crazy as a jay bird."

"Would you say this Professor Snelf had any interest in the ivory ibis?"

"I'll say. He was charmed with the whole idea. He even dressed up as an ibis for the faculty Halloween party. Imagine that! It wasn't a very good costume. He made it himself. Looked more like a polar bear or something. Something with a long nose."

"Did Snelf believe in the treasure story nonsense?"

"Oh, who knows? He's never serious. Everything's a joke to Dr. Snelf. Still, I can't see him doing anything violent, like dropping Dr. Lund out a window. Too much of a milquetoast for that."

"What about Lund? Has she made any enemies on campus?"

"I shouldn't talk about her. She gave me a very nice wood carving last Christmas. A little pony. I always wanted a pony as a child. But where are my manners? Can I offer you some coffee or anything? Perhaps some cookies?"

"I'm fine, thank you. Listen, this ibis business is serious. If there's anything you can tell me about Kirsten Lund that might help me get to the bottom of this matter, you owe it to everyone to spill your guts."

"I suppose that's true. Well, Dr. Lund is what my mother would have called no better than she should be."

"Oh? A little hellion is she?"

"Not exactly that. Passionate. Overly passionate. She's been involved with a number of our professors over the years"

"Including Dr. Crampton?"

"Dear, yes. They were quite the couple for a time. I heard they sometimes stayed over at each other's places."

"Scandalous! All night, you mean? And these are the people teaching our children?"

"I know. It's a shock. In my day, such a thing would have been impossible."

"I know. Back then professors behaved pretty much like priests and nuns."

"I don't know about that, but they didn't sleep over. And they kept their hands off the students."

"Crampton and Lund get cozy with their students?"

"I don't know about Dr. Crampton, but there's been talk about Dr. Lund being romantically involved with a certain boy."

"Is that boy still around?"

"No. He graduated. I believe he got 'A's from Dr. Lund, though he wasn't that good a student."

"What about this Dr. Umbray, the dish? Is she hot to trot?"

"No. She's nicknamed the Ice Queen, poor dear. Though there's talk she and Dr. Crampton are an item."

"I see. And this Ollie Crampton is out of town, so I hear. Off in New Mexico working on a dig."

"He's always on sabbatical it seems. Though he's quite respectable and is considered a good teacher."

"But he dumped Lund for Umbray?"

"I wouldn't put it that way."

"Let me ask you something else. Are you going to the English Department Christmas party tonight?"

"No. I'm always invited, but I don't go. I went once. There was plenty of punch and eggnog. Spiked. Things got a bit out of hand."

"Happy to hear it. I'm going to this year's party. I'm Eben Mulford's date."

She raised her eyebrows.

"I've heard he might be that sort. A man his age, never married. What else could you think?"

"I honestly don't know if Eben walks on that side of the street, but I'm getting my magenta taffeta gown out of moth balls just in case."

"Now you're making fun of me."

"I wouldn't do that. Do you think Snelf will be at the party?"

"That's a given. He'll probably bring his own lamp shade."

"A big party boy, is he? I look forward to meeting him." I stood up. "Thank you for your time, Minnie. You've given me some ideas. I appreciate your help. Can I call on you again if I need to?"

"Yes, of course. I'll try to have the place cleaned up for you next time. I'm afraid I'm not much of a housekeeper."

"You live alone. What difference does it make? I'll find my own way to the door. Thanks."

I sat in my car a while, trying to decide what I

should do next. Minnie hadn't really helped much, though I was interested in meeting this guy, Snelf. I thought maybe I'd drop over to the college library where the original ivory ibis had been stolen from the museum.

I should have asked Minnie where the library was located, but I figured I could find it myself. I drove the short distance to the campus and looked around for a building that looked like a library. I spotted one that looked like a fixed-up Roman ruin. Sure enough, it was the library. I went in. The place was pretty deserted. I found an old crone with half-eye reading glasses and a too-large sweater who was sitting behind a big desk in the lobby area.

"Could you direct me to the museum?" I asked her.

"Are you a member of the faculty?"

"No, I'm a private dick. A shamus. A gumshoe. I don't even read, believe me. I'm investigating the theft of a piece of ancient Egyptian art. Some kind of bird. Maybe a duck."

"Does this have to do with Dr. Lund's attack?"

"Oh, you've heard about that? Sure. I'll lay my cards on the table. I'm looking into the Lund misfortune. I thought I'd talk to the museum curator if I may."

"You'll find him in Arkansas. He traveled there for Christmas. But I have the key to the museum. We've kept it locked since the theft. Do you have some identification I can see?"

I worked one of my business cards out of my wallet and handed it to the old harridan. She read it out loud. I was disappointed; I thought librarians could read without moving their lips.

"'Axel Hatchett. Private Investigator. No Nut Too Hard To Crack.' Do you have anything else?"

"Driver's license. Blood donor card. Gas card. A picture of me in my Cub Scout uniform. Which of those would you like to see?"

She made a sour face.

"Come this way."

I followed her sensible shoes across the lobby and down a corridor and finally to a locked door. She took a key ring from her sweater pocket and unlocked for me.

"Thanks," I said. "Can I just look around, or do you have to follow me?"

"The museum is available for your private perusal. When you're finished, please let me know so that I can lock up again."

"Swell. Thanks."

She disappeared and I made the tour of the museum. I could see why Kirsten Lund had made fun of the place. It was basically a junk shop. There was a glass display case with some kind of dusty mummy in it. It looked like a monkey that'd been forgotten in the hospital. There was the skeleton of a horse, nicely articulated, in the middle of the floor. There was a display of all kinds of arrowheads and spear points collected locally. There were parchment scrolls, paintings on bark, some old medicine bottles, a miniature replica of a Venetian gondola, some glass beads.

There were maps, some badly restored oil paintings, and there was a big display of carved figures from all over the globe. A couple of them were Egyptian, and there was a conspicuous — almost accusatory — blank space with a card that read: "Ancient Egyptian Ivory Ibis — The God Thoth. Questionable Authenticity. Donated by Dr. Kirsten Lund." I looked at the blank space for a while and it told me nothing.

I left the wonders of the museum and sought the cranky librarian again.

"Do you guys have any idea who stole that dingus? The bird?"

She stood up and got the keys out of her sweater again.

"Follow me," she said.

I followed her back to the museum and watched her lock up.

"The police and campus security have no idea who stole the figure," she told me. "It couldn't have been taken during the day; the top of the display case was shattered. A noise of breaking glass would have been noticed. This is, after all, a library. Someone likely hid out in the building until after closing time. The library doors can only be opened with a key, and they're doubtless far harder to pick than the museum door.

"The thief, whoever it was, broke into the museum during the night, smashed the display case, and acquired the Egyptian artifact. 'The bird,' as you call it. 'The dingus.' Then they had to stay here until the library was unlocked in the morning."

"They spent the night here? That's commitment."

"For a very unworthy purpose. Can I help you with anything else — Mr.?"

"Hatchett. Axe Hatchett."

"Brutal name. It fits. Good evening, then."

I left the library. I didn't know what my next step should be, but I was looking forward to the English Department Christmas party. I stopped by my office to see if anyone had pinned a note to my door. I don't have a phone answering service yet. Maybe when I get more money. There were no notes. I looked around my office for no particular reason. It was dusty and musty smelling, and the overpowering stench of the ice cream shop below my office was as noxious as ever. I drove home.

On the way I decided to have a decent dinner so I wouldn't make a pig of myself with the swell hors d'oeuvres at the party. That left out Rocko's. I stopped at a lunch counter and consumed a pretty decent hot roast beef sandwich and some coffee and apple pie.

When I got home I checked the mail. Bills. I stretched out on my bed and thought about Crosby Dumpler. Was it possible he was behind the ivory ibis crime? What he'd said about not wanting to abandon his practice while he went off to

Egypt made sense. But he could send a partner. I only wished I hadn't given in to Tracy and Eben. If they hadn't been along for the interview I might have made out better with Dumpler. He might have let something slip.

But I was also bothered by the condition of Lund's apartment. Nothing broken. It made no sense.

But her throwing herself out of a window didn't make sense either. Maybe it had been an accident. Maybe she had planned on landing on that heap of leaves below her attic window. But why would she concoct such a phony crime? What could she get out of that? Sympathy? Attention? She didn't seem the sort to want either. What did she have to gain by pretending someone wanted that damned ibis? And how had Ollie Crampton's ibis gone missing?

I supposed Lund could have taken it. If she and Ollie had been lovers, she might still have a key to his place. And she could have also stolen the bird from the library museum. So much for opportunity. But I had no clue what her motive could be.

The green-eyed monster might have had its hand in the matter. But how would faking a robbery that involved a fake treasure map help Kirsten hurt her rival, Lilith? There could be an answer, but I didn't have it.

7

I got ready for the drunken bacchanal at Dean Gallcarver's. After I changed, I called Eben.

Eben doesn't usually answer his phone, but I figured his concern for Lund might temporarily change his habits. He answered.

"So, do I need to bring anything to this little party?" I asked him.

"You mean a bottle of wine? A bouquet of flowers? Cheese dip, pretzels, that sort of thing?"

"Yeah, that's right."

"No, but I'll leave it up to you. You can be your usual gauche self and bring nothing. No one will notice."

"Good, because flowers and cheese dip don't grow on trees, you know."

"Actually, some trees do grow flowers."

"Sure, be an expert, see if I care. Heard anything from Lund?"

"I visited Kirsten in the hospital again. She's practically gnashing her teeth. She can't tolerate inaction. Imagine how she feels being flat on her back in the hospital, unable to so much as walk?"

"I guess it's tough on her."

"Did you find Minnie?"

"Yeah. I even got a look at her bra and girdle."

"I won't ask for details."

"She's a sloppy housekeeper is all. She couldn't help me much, though she got me interested in Dr. Snelf. What's his first name? Ray?"

"Correct. Why are you interested in him?"

"Minnie said he was pretty damned interested in the ivory ibis treasure story."

"As a joke, nothing more."

"We'll see."

"You'll be meeting him tonight."

"So I heard. He'll be the guy spiking the punch, right?"

"No doubt someone will spike it. That's part of the fun at the annual Christmas party at Dean Gallcarver's. That might be the only fun. There will be a lot of posturing and toadying going on. The Dean enjoys such tribute."

"Will Lilith be there?"

"I can't say. She is distinctly less sycophantic than some of the other professors, but she might show up. Are you hoping for that?"

"Sure."

"Don't forget the charming young lady you're engaged to."

"You really think Tracy's charming? I thought you were just feeding her compliments."

"She glows like a firefly. She has character and spirit. You don't deserve her."

"I won't argue with any of that, but if you could see her at Rocko's, slinging hash, you might have a different opinion about her charm."

"By all means, please help her find a different position."

"I'll go work on that. What should I be wearing tonight?"

"Jacket, tie, pressed trousers, unscuffed shoes. Can you manage all that?"

"Sure. Like I was dressed when you saw me this morning?"

"Yes, although there was a distinct prune-like quality to your clothing."

"OK, so I'll heat up the old iron" I didn't tell him that I was already dressed. So much for the old iron. "And I'll bring my copy of Bartlett's Familiar Quotations so I can keep up my end of the conversation. See you around seven."

"You can be late. Everyone else will be. It's a department tradition."

I basically sat around the house for a while longer. Then I heard my neighbor come home. I glanced out the window to make sure it was Blythe's Pontiac, and when I saw it was her, I headed outdoors. Time to check on the kittens and ask a question or two.

"You home at this hour?" she greeted me. "I thought a private eye's work was never done."

"A guy's got to take a break now and then. Can

I see my kittens?"

"You may. Come on in. Stay away from Mama Cat, though. She was in a mood this morning."

"She's probably ready to send the kids out to find jobs. Busy day at work?"

"Not so much. It's been a pretty quiet Christmas season. Hardly any domestic violence cases. I'm not sure what that means."

"It means we've all decided to embrace peace and joy, like the season teaches us."

"Somehow, Axe, you've been getting too much sun."

I followed her into her cottage. It was spotless, as always. It made me fear she didn't have enough of a social life. The kittens were everywhere. There seemed to be at least a dozen of them instead of just five. Blythe picked one off the living room drapes, rescued another from being drowned in the water dish by its sibling, and pulled another out of the kitchen wastebasket.

"I swear, Mama has given up on raising her children," she said.

"Maybe she thinks they're perfect just the way they are."

"She's sure wrong about that."

I tracked down and corralled my two fur balls. I think the ornery one was the kitten that was trying to drown his brother or sister. They squirmed and mewed in my arms, then settled down and let me pet them. I wondered what Tracy would name them.

"Offer you a beer?" asked Blythe.

"No thanks. Have one for me."

"I will." She returned from the fridge with a Black Label in one hand and a kitten in the other.

"In the midst of your busy police life," I started, "did you happen to hear about a strange accident? Seems a couple of guys were looking for a treasure map and dangled an English professor out an attic window to make her tell where she'd hidden it. They dropped her and she broke her leg."

"Yes, I heard about that one." She made it sound like a joke she'd heard once too often. "What about it? Did somebody hire you to track down the assailants?"

"Yes, but I'm not getting very far."

"It only happened last night."

"Sure, but this is Axe Hatchett, private sleuth, were talking about."

"Excuse me for underestimating your prowess."

"Prowess? You dating a guy with a thesaurus?"

"Not dating anyone. My secret admirer still hasn't revealed himself."

"Maybe it's the Chief of Police."

"Let's hope not. I can't stand the skunk."

"Then chances are he's your secret admirer. Have you heard anything about that case that you could share with your favorite neighbor?"

"Don't think so."

"The case sounds a little screwy to me."

"I'll say. But I can't help you."

"Did you cops notice anything funny about the crime scene?"

"I wasn't there, honey. They don't let me have that much fun. What was funny about it?"

"The whole joint was torn apart, but not a damned thing was broken."

"Were there a lot of breakables?"

"I'll say. A whole bunch of fragile carvings. They were all over the floor, but not a one had a mark on it. What do you think?"

"Maybe those two guys are just naturally gentle."

"Yeah. Gentle enough to dangle a woman out of an attic window, and then drop her."

"What's your take on it?"

"I think it was a set-up. I'm inclined to believe the victim planned the whole thing herself, but I'm damned if I can figure out why."

"Keep working on it. That powerful mind of yours will come up with something, even if it don't fit the facts."

"Thanks for your confidence. Listen, I've got to go. I'm heading out for a party."

"Lucky you. Taking your cutie out to have some Christmas fun?"

"No. This is work."

"Poor thing. Your job's nothing but a trial and a misery. Have fun. What are you going to name your new kids?"

"I'll leave that up to Tracy. Enjoy your beer. See

you later."

Eben was waiting for me, standing on the steps of his quaint porch, dressed in a dark suit and a string tie.

"I knew you'd be early," he said. "You are always quite the early bird."

"I've developed a taste for worms"

"You look quite respectable. Let us walk very slowly. Really, we don't want to be the first guests. Dean Gallcarver is considered a brilliant scholar — his area is seventeenth century Welsh closet comedies — but his conversation is pedestrian at best. And his wife, Deidre is, well, you'll see."

So we walked very slowly down the uneven walks for two blocks, talking quietly together.

"I thought perhaps I would not mention your true profession tonight," said Eben. "I thought you might wish to remain incognito."

"That's a good idea. It's not always wise to let folks know you're a detective. They clam up."

"Yes. And I don't want you to become the center of attention. Detectives are quite popular now, you know."

"Happy to hear it. It's nice to be liked."

"I thought I'd introduce you as an insurance adjuster."

"That's good. Nice and dull. But you're forgetting that Lilith has already met me. She knows I'm a detective."

"We'll give her a heads up. I'm sure she'll cooperate, if she shows up."

My heart slithered down to my shoes. "You really think she might not show?"

"As I told you, she is less political than many of her peers. But—who knows?—she might not have anything more interesting to do tonight. Walk a little slower, please. We're in sight of the Gallcarver's and I don't see any cars parked out front."

"Maybe everybody walked, like us."

"Not likely. Kirsten was talking of stealing a wheelchair and joining us here. That would be a terrific distance for a wheelchair. I do wish she would simply accept her situation and not chafe at it so much. Hello, what's this?"

He pointed ahead and I saw a dusty Willys station wagon pull up at the curb half a block in front of us.

"That's Ollie Crampton's vehicle," said Eben, "I'm sure of it."

"I thought he was still in New Mexico."

"So did I. Odd. What's odder is that he's crashing an English Department Christmas party. I'm sure he'll be welcome, but why would anyone want to do such a thing?"

"Maybe he's hoping to meet Lilith here."

"That is a possibility. Wait — look. What's he getting out of the back of his station wagon?"

"Looks like a wheelchair. You don't think — ?"

"Yes, that's exactly what I think."

We stood and watched as Ollie unloaded the wheel chair, unfolded it into position, and rolled it over to the passenger's side of his car. He opened the door, bent down, and scooped out his passenger, Kirsten Lund. She had managed to put on an ocean-blue dress and one high-heeled shoe. Her leg cast glowed bright white in the light from the nearest street lamp. Ollie placed her in the chair and pushed it along the front walk that led, I presumed, to Dean Gallcarver's hulking Victorian house with its two front turrets. Eben and I let out our breaths at the same time and resumed our walk.

"She's insane. Her upper leg is broken. It's dangerous for her to be out like this. A bit of bone marrow could get into her bloodstream and stop her heart. I know of such a case. How irresponsible of Ollie to help her in such madness."

"Some folks just won't take no for an answer. This could prove to be an interesting night."

We went up the porch steps and rang the bell. A mostly-bald man, close to sixty I would guess, wearing a green sweater and a red tie, opened the door for us.

"Merry Christmas, Duncan. This is my friend, Axe Hatchett. He expressed an interest in your little entertainment tonight, so I brought him along."

Duncan Gallcarver stuck out a fishy paw and I briefly clamped down on it.

"Merry Christmas, and welcome, Mr. Hatchett."

"Call me Axe. Nice to meet you."

"We have only two other guests so far," said the Dean.

"Yes," said Eben, "we saw them enter. I simply can't believe that Kirsten would leave the hospital. She doesn't know what's good for her."

"Maybe the party will cheer her up," said Gall-carver.

We entered an entry hall and hung our coats and hats on a big coat rack. Then we wiped our feet on a fake Persian carpet and followed the Dean into a large, high-ceilinged, living room. It was all decorated for Christmas, and there was a big tree in one corner adorned with what looked like antique ornaments.

Two long, cloth-covered, tables displayed trays and dishes of various snacks, and there was a big punch bowl full of something red, and a smaller bowl filled with eggnog. A silver coffee urn with cups arranged around it took up the end of one table.

A half-drowned looking woman, about the same age as the Dean, was doing her best to dampen the effect of her cheery red dress. She was talking to Ollie and Kirsten, her face a vague frowning mask. She kept gazing around the room as if the conversation wasn't of much interest to her. The Dean hurried us forward for introductions.

8

"This is my wife, Deidre, and Kirsten Lund, and Ollie Crampton."

"So pleased," breathed Deidre, her eyes tracking around my head like I had gnats in my hair. She seemed heavily drugged.

"Dr. Lund and I have met," I said. "You must be a remarkable healer," I said to her.

"That hospital would have killed me," she said. "Fortunately, Ollie drove all the way up from New Mexico to rescue me."

"She called me long distance at five o'clock this morning," complained Ollie, although good naturedly. He looked like a weather-beaten Cary Grant, but likely not as tall. He wore the professor's uniform of a shabby sports coat and baggy pants. He wore no tie. "I just happened to be at the ranch house I've been using as my bivouac while I was out on my dig. I spend most of my nights at the dig site, in my tent. But yesterday the weather turned too cold even for me, and we had some snow. I slept at the ranch house last night. Or tried to." He gave Kirsten a sarcastic grin.

"I woke up the rancher at five this morning and told him I had to reach Ollie Crampton, that it was a matter of life and death."

"Which it clearly was not," said Ollie. "Although, actually, I did fear for the lives of the nurses and doctors who were trying to tell Kirsten what to do. So I drove up here and rescued them from her. I was seven-hundred miles away. It took me over ten hours to get here, and I thought the Willys was going to give up the ghost. But, here I am. Here we are."

"How ever did you talk the hospital staff into letting you go?" Eben asked Kirsten.

"I didn't ask them. Ollie brought over his mother's old wheel chair that he had stored in his garage, and we simply left. I'll settle my bill later."

"You are incorrigible," said Eben.

"Well, dear Eben, I couldn't miss this party, now could I?"

Eben turned to Ollie. "I would like to reprimand you, sir, for your part in helping Kirsten to escape her medical helpers."

"We could fight a duel." suggested Ollie, with a big smile. "You know how Kirsten is. If I hadn't helped her, somebody else would have. She was determined."

Dr. Lund was putting on a good show, but she was clearly in pain. Her face was as white as her cast, and she winced every time she wriggled in her wheel chair. I hoped she hadn't done any damage to her leg.

Ollie was quick to engage me in conversation. He was a likable guy.

"Mr. Hatchett, you don't look foolish enough to belong to the academic community. What do you do for a living?"

"I'm a snoop, a peeper. I work as a private investigator. Freelance."

Ollie winked and poked a thumb at me. "I knew you were a detective. Kirs mentioned you to me. I was just seeing if you were working under cover, trying to pass yourself off as an encyclopedia salesman or some such."

"I'd considered saying I was an insurance adjuster."

"That's even worse. I'm glad you aren't incognito. Now I can talk to you about your profession. Say, do you carry a gun?"

"Sometimes."

"I hope you're carrying one tonight. I know this crowd." He turned away and shouted at Eben. "That eggnog won't do you any good. It hasn't been spiked yet."

I turned and saw Eben jump. He had his back to us. I walked over to see what was up.

"Why the jitters?" I whispered to him.

"Hush. Watch my back." He took a large silver flask from an inside coat pocket, unscrewed the cap, and poured the contents into the eggnog bowl.

"So you're the culprit," I said. "Minnie told me the libations at this affair were a hundred proof."

"It's the only way to get through the evening. I'm not the only person who spikes the drinks. I brought bourbon. I hope someone else will bring vodka for the fruit punch. Or rum."

"I'll stick with coffee. Just between you and me, your friend Kirsten doesn't look so good."

"The poor fool. Why must she be so willful? I'm sure there's no way we'll get her back into the hospital now."

"She can't stay at her place. What about the stairs?"

"I've been talking to her. She has things all worked out. Ollie will move back into his place and Lilith will occupy Kirsten's apartment. Kirsten will stay downstairs in Minnie's place. Minnie doesn't have a guest room, so Ollie will move a bed down from upstairs and set it up in Minnie's living room. Quite an imposition for Minnie, but she's agreed to it."

"I guess that arrangement will work. Speaking of Lilith, where is she?"

"You do have a weakness for delectable females. Would you like to call her and ask her if she's coming?"

"No. But you could do that for me. What's up with the Dean's wife? Is she a morphine addict?"

"Not an addict, no, but she does take narcotics. She has an extremely nervous temperament. There's a story that's gone the rounds of the department for years. According to rumor, Deidre once went after Duncan with a sledge hammer, simply because he was being too noisy with a stapler."

"Sounds like a little more than mere nervousness."

"Well, the Dean has a reputation to protect. Crazy wives aren't allowed to be called crazy."

"Swell household. Any kids?"

"All grown up and moved away. Doubtless, their childhoods were not idyllic."

"I'm going to have some of this food. But I'm not turning my back on Deidre."

"Wise resolve. I'm going to sample this eggnog."

I don't know who all I met that night. For the next half-hour, professors and their guests trickled in, the latest arrivals full of Christmas cheer of the liquid variety. For the most part they clustered around the Dean and his somnambulist wife. Even Lund, whom I didn't think of as a toady, stuck pretty close to Gallcarver and laughed too loud and too often. Of course, Ollie couldn't care less what the Dean of the English department thought of him. And Lilith, when she finally arrived, stuck with Ollie and me and Eben, and the Snelfs, when they showed up.

Ray Snelf was a character. So was his wife, Cassie. Ray brought a flask of gin to pour into the otherwise dull punch, but he didn't need the stimulus. He seemed genuinely happy to be there. And

after paying his respects to his host — and boss —
Dean Gallcarver, he circulated around and ended
up talking to me. He was delighted to discover
that I was a detective.

"You don't look like Sherlock Holmes," he told
me, "or my idea of C. Auguste Dupin. You must
be one of these American thunderbolts I've heard
about. Perhaps you're another Sam Spade, or the
Continental Op, or maybe Philip Marlow."

"I'm not any of those. Just a poor working
stiff."

"He carries a gun," Ollie pointed out.

"Terrific! Can I see it?" asked Snelf.

"I left it at home," I lied.

"What kind is it?"

"Well, my normal carry gun is a snub-nosed
thirty-eight. A Chief's Special. But sometimes I
back it up with a Browning High Power in nine
millimeter."

"Wonderful. I wish we professors could carry
guns. Should we ask the Dean for permission? I
think it would improve our students' attendance
and attention."

"I doubt if the Dean would allow it," observed
Eben.

"Stuffed shirt. Spoil sport." He said this in a
whisper.

"So, what do you think about your colleague
getting attacked by treasure hunters?" I asked
Snelf.

"Sinister and ominous. But that's the curse of

the ivory ibis for you. I warned Kirsten to get rid of those copies she made. Those goons who attacked her obviously believed she had the real goods. She's lucky they didn't part her pretty head from her pretty neck."

"Do you believe in the story of the ivory ibis?" I asked. "I mean, do you think there's anything behind the legend?"

"Why, of course. A story as good as that one couldn't be fake. It's wonderful. I'm sure if that map were found, the treasure of King Tut would look like a pawn shop collection. I just wish I had that map."

"You'd go off to Egypt, would you?" I asked.

"No, he wouldn't," said Cassie. "If Ray had that map he'd put it someplace safe and no one would ever see it again"

"She's probably right," admitted Ray. "But I'd be smart. I'd make a copy of it and give it to Eben for safe keeping."

"Why me?"

"Those snakes of yours would protect it from thieves. There'd be no use dangling those snakes out of attic windows. They wouldn't hiss out the secret to anyone. Not if I know my serpents."

"All you know about snakes is that they don't have legs," said Eben.

"Yes, no legs. And forked tongues. Or is it forked tails?"

"Do you think anyone besides yourself believes the tale of the ivory ibis is genuine?" I persisted.

"Of course. I'm certain Lilith here gives the legend credence. That's why she hid away Ollie's own ivory ibis, pretending that it had been stolen."

"Oh, is that what I did?" laughed Lilith.

"You did. And when you show up in a classroom all decked out in valuable Egyptian jewels and gold, we'll all know the truth."

"After I take my sabbatical in Egypt?"

"Don't forget your pith helmet, with a veil attached. That skin of yours wasn't meant to brave the sun in the land of hippos and crocodiles."

I could see I wasn't going to get any serious comments out of Snelf. I shifted gears and concentrated on the play between Ollie, Kirsten, and Lilith. The deadly triangle: more dangerous than crocodiles and hippos combined. When Lilith had entered, she had gone straight to Kirsten and had spent a few moments talking to her. However, the expressions on the two women's faces hadn't indicated any great friendship. Clenched teeth and false smiles were the order of the day. Then Lilith had drifted over to Ollie, where she stayed for most of the rest of the evening.

Ollie was pleasant and playful with her, but there was no sign that he had any passionate feelings for her. But he was an old hand at this game, from what I'd heard. I eavesdropped a little. I really am a peeper.

"Well, good Sir Arthur," said Lilith to Ollie, "it was very brave and bold of you to come to your damsel's rescue."

"She's not my damsel. And you forgot to mention my noble steed, the well-born Willys."

"Would you drive so many miles, and at such a furious pace, to rescue little old me?"

"Of course, but I wouldn't need to. Little old you is quite capable of taking care of yourself."

"Can I keep your gun a little longer? I don't like the idea of Kirsten and me living in the same house with those beastly treasure hunters hot on our trail."

"But all the ibises are accounted for, Lilith. The whole flock."

"No. The one stolen from our fine museum is still missing. And what about the map?"

"It never existed."

"There are at least two people who disagree with you. Besides, I may need the revolver to defend myself from Kirsten. You know how she hates me, and why."

"Because your career is going decidedly better than hers?"

"That too. When will I be seeing you?"

"You can drop by any time. I won't be doing anything but avoiding my family."

"It's too bad you had to return early."

"True, but just between you and me, my dig wasn't going too well. I wasn't finding the right things, and I was finding too many of the wrong things. It's humbling for me to have to give up a pet theory, but that's how it is."

"I'm so sorry. Back to the drawing board, eh?"

"Yes, and I'll need plenty of chalk this time."

"If I leave Kirsten's house late at night, she'll know where I'm going."

"What's she going to do, chase you down in her wheelchair?"

"Maybe. Thank God she can't drive. Can she?'

"With that leg in a cast? Impossible. Maybe you'll get lucky and the thieves will return and finish her off."

"I can't believe you'd say such a thing. That's awful."

"But wouldn't we both be better off?"

"We'll both be better off if we find some other man for her to concentrate on."

"Yes, but whom?"

"Maybe that awful detective who's goggling at us."

They laughed. I stopped goggling.

But it wasn't easy to not stare at Lilith. She was wearing a long red dress with black satin trim. The dress embraced her perfect figure perfectly. Her long wavy hair was combed out over her back and shoulders, with a few thick tendrils caressing her face. There were two red ribbons in her brown hair. She was a jewel, a vision. Stuff like that.

As the night wore on, more eggnog and punch were consumed. Voices got louder, jokes got sillier, serious observations took on the importance of life and death situations. I don't care much for drunken parties, and I didn't think there was much more for me to find out from these people. The attack of the ivory ibis liberators was still very much a mystery. I suggested to Eben that we say our goodbyes to our hosts and fellow guests and hit the road.

"Gladly." He replied.

We walked back to Eben's happy home. He'd had more eggnog than was good for him, and staggered a little, though in a very dignified way.

"Thank God it's over," he said.

"It wasn't as bad as all that."

"Perhaps I've seen too many such parties. Always the same groveling, the same false cheer. And later, once the enhanced holiday libations have had their effect, the same petty bickering, the same clumsy attempts at amour."

"You don't have to go. You're retired."

"Perhaps I won't go next year. Did you get anything out of it at all?"

"I'm not sure. I'll have to think things through. I believe you're right about Snelf, though. He's a joker; he doesn't take the ivory ibis seriously. But I may have picked up a thing or two I can use. I hope Dr. Lund gets home OK."

"She was drinking, did you notice? It'll throw off her coordination. She might spill from her wheelchair."

"I think Ollie will take care of her."

"Good old Ollie. A woman's best friend."

"You seem pretty bitter for a guy who's full of eggnog."

"Not bitter, tired. Nothing changes. Nothing in this world changes."

"Go pet your snakes. Get a good night's sleep. Stay in bed until noon tomorrow."

"All good advice."

We were in front of his house.

"Good night, old man," he said. "Solve this case for me, please. I feel the weight of doom hanging over Kirsten. Surely she won't be attacked again."

"She'll be with Minnie and Lilith. She'll be all right. If you want, I can have an operative watch her house at nights."

"I think that's a wonderful plan."

"I'll call Bram Duckers when I get home."

"Call him from my place, by all means."

"None of your snakes are loose, are they?"

"Only Constance, and she's very small. A coral snake. Lovely stripes."

"Keep her away from me while I use your phone. If you like stripes, why didn't you get a zebra?"

"They're noisy, smelly, bad tempered, and they eat too much, not to mention knocking over the furniture."

We went inside and I got on the horn. I dialed Bram's number and listened to his phone ring about a hundred times. Damn it! The guy and his wife and baby were probably out of town, visiting relatives in this time of festivity. Why couldn't people stay home when I needed them? I tried to think of someone I trusted who had extra time and needed money. I couldn't think of anybody. I'd have to do it myself, and that meant I'd have to make another phone call.

I dialed the number for Rocko's Kitchen. It was close to midnight, so the joint was closed, but Tracy lived in a couple of rooms above Rocko's. She didn't have her own phone, but she'd hear the phone downstairs if I let it ring enough times.

"Hello? We're closed. Are you nuts?"

"It's me, lemon rind. Sorry to wake you up."

"Wake me up any time, my little pearl onion. It's always good to hear your manly voice."

"Swell. Listen, I just wanted you to know I'll be out of pocket for a while. I'm on the night shift. I'll be watching Kirsten Lund's house for a couple of nights."

"Has something happened?"

"No, and I hope things stay that way."

"Why don't you get that guy Bram to watch her place?"

"I tried calling him and the bum didn't answer. Probably out of town."

"You can't think of anyone else to help you?"

"No, nobody I trust."

"Let me do it."

"You? No, you've got a day job."

"Let Miss Priss do my job. I'm telling you, I've about had it with her and Cookie."

"I understand, but don't give up your job just yet. We both need to be working right now. We're saving up for an apartment and a honeymoon, remember? Not to mention a wedding. How's the wisdom tooth?"

"Sore. I go to the dentist tomorrow."

"Good. Listen, I've got to go. I'll be sleeping tomorrow, so don't wake me if you don't have to."

"You don't want to hear my sweet voice?"

"Not when I'm sleeping. Good night, ginger muffin."

"Good night, my little pork chop."

I told Eben what the arrangement was going to be.

"That's unfortunate. You need your sleep."

"I'll be all right. I had nothing but coffee at the party. Which reminds me, can I avail myself of your lovely powder room? Constance isn't in there, is she? I don't want to disturb her."

"I believe she's under the china cupboard. Silly girl."

"Yeah. Those coral snakes are a riot."

9

I parked my car across the street and half a block down from Lund's house at a little before twelve thirty. Ollie's Willys was parked out front, along with Minnie's Dodge, and a cute little Muntz convertible that must have been Lilith's ride. There were lights in the ground floor and upstairs windows. I figured Ollie must be helping set up Kirsten's bed in Minnie's living room. I had nothing but time on my hands — nothing to do but think — so that's what I did.

Had Ollie tried to kill Kirsten because she was being a difficult former lover? That seemed excessive, unless she had something on him. He had a history of wooing and tossing women aside. Maybe there was a hidden scandal or two that the college didn't know everything about, something that could threaten his job. A knocked-up student, a teaching assistant's suicide? When you rest your head on the pillow next to your lover's, you learn things about them. And not just that they snore.

But if Ollie had used the ivory ibis story to arrange Kirsten's death, he hadn't been one of her midnight visitors. He had talked on the phone with Kirsten at five o'clock in the morning, only a few hours after Lund had been attacked. He was seven-hundred miles away from Quartz Quarry; that much could be proved. Unless he'd hired an airplane and a pilot to fly him to our fair city and back to his archeology dig.

Not likely. That sort of thing can be checked on. And the weather had probably been too bad for flying.

Of course, Ollie could have hired a couple of thugs—students, for that matter—to be his henchmen. He could have figured a way to keep out of the picture, maybe handling most of the business by phone. It was a possibility, but there were others.

I tried on Lilith for size as the potential murderer. She knew all about the ivory ibis, and was in a position to keep pretty close track of Lund's movements. She would have to have had a helper, and how a girl like her could have disguised herself as a man I couldn't imagine. But she, like Ollie, could have employed hired help. Hell, all she would have to do was bat her dusky eyelashes and I would have done the job myself.

I was beginning to nod off. I turned the car radio on but I couldn't get a station at that time of night. Just static. But static was annoying enough to keep me awake for a while.

Around one-thirty, Ollie came out of the house, climbed into his Willys, and disappeared. Presumably he was on his way home. In a few minutes more the house lights went out. Folks were going to bed. That's what I wanted to do, too. I blinked my eyes a few times and shook my head back and forth.

Then a car, its headlights dimmed, came creeping up the street, coming in my direction. That woke me up. The streetlights showed me a Chevy, a beat up one, probably black or dark blue. It was too dark to tell which. The car's low speed had nothing to do with the weather. It wasn't icy or even snowy on the streets.

It stopped right across from Lund's house, and then sat there with its motor running. I could see the exhaust rising in the light from the street lamps. In about five minutes, the car lurched into motion, picked up speed, and drove past me. I waited a few seconds, made a U-turn, and headed off in pursuit.

I stayed well behind the car, but I don't think the driver was watching his rearview mirror. I cursed myself for not having switched cars with Tracy. Her old brown Chevrolet was a lot less conspicuous than my crimson Nash Airflyte. But there was nothing I could do about it now.

We drove on for about two miles, turning onto different streets twice. Finally, after we'd entered a low-rent part of town, the car in front of me slowed down and parked at the curb in front of an old two-storied house.

I kept driving. My headlights briefly lit up the Chevy's license plate and I memorized the number. I also noticed the house. There were five mailboxes mounted next to the front door. The old place had been turned into apartments. It was a good place for starving college students to live. Most of the Flinders College kids were pretty well-heeled, but that wasn't true of all of them. I suspected I had just stumbled upon Kirsten Lund's attackers.

My first impulse was to go on home and get some sleep. But I'd promised Eben I would keep an eye on his friend's house, so I drove back to Lund's place and parked where I'd parked before. Nothing happened.

I fought sleep until the cold morning sun lit-up the overcast sky, and then I drove home to my little cabin. I took in the mail — bills — undressed, and went to bed. I slept for several hours, got up and had some coffee and eggs, and planned my next move. It was eleven o'clock. I called the Quartz Quarry Police Department and asked to speak to Officer Blythe Bliss.

"This is Bliss."

"Blythe, this is Axe."

"The kittens are fine. They're growing."

"Happy to hear it. Listen, can you do me a favor? Can you run a license plate number for me?"

"That's not my job."

"Could you ask whoever's job it is to run a

number for me?" I gave her the number. "Can you call me back on this?"

"I'm just your little girl Friday, aren't I?"

"You're mean when you're at work. Come on, who else should I be asking? We're neighbors, re-member? And I seem to recall doing you a favor or two in the past."

"OK, don't get grumpy. I'll run the number and call you back. You at your office?"

"No, I'm still home. I'll be here for another hour or so."

"I'll give you a call."

I called Eben next.

"I hope I didn't wake you."

"No, I'm eating my breakfast."

"Feeling all right?"

"A bit queasy, but I'll be all right. What's the word?"

"Somebody in a beat-up Chevy stopped in front of Dr. Lund's house about three o'clock this morn-ing. They didn't do anything, just sat in front of the house for about five minutes, then took off again. I followed them and got the license number. The house they parked at looked like it might be a hangout for starving college students."

"Wonderful. It sounds like you're on the trail of the villains."

"Let's hope so. I'm following up on it. I just thought I'd let you know what's going on."

"Thank you, Axe."

I hung up and called Rocko's. A lovely voice

answered the phone.

"Can I speak to Tracy, Prissy May? It's Axe Hatchett."

"She's out smoking. I'll get her, Mr. Hatchett."

Smoking? Tracy doesn't smoke. It was a good two minutes before Tracy came to the phone.

"Hello, lamb chop," she greeted me.

"Don't give me that. What are you doing smoking?"

"I just took it up. I couldn't help it. Prissy May's driving me crazy."

"That's no excuse. No more smoking for you. It's a filthy habit."

"You smoke cigars."

"That's because I'm a chump. Promise me you won't smoke anymore."

"All right. I only bummed a couple of cigarettes off Cookie, that's all."

"Next time Prissy May gets on your nerves, chew on a rag or something."

"I'll try it."

"Only don't use that favorite rag of yours you wipe down the counters with. That'd be worse than smoking."

"OK. Did you get enough sleep? It's only eleven thirty. What time did you get home?"

"Seven. I'm all right. I'll be working on the case all day, so you might not hear from me."

"Stop by Rocko's sometime. You still need to eat."

"Yeah, well, change your smock and gargle

some of that battery acid you sell instead of coffee. If I stop by, I'm going to sniff your breath and your clothes to make sure you aren't smoking."

"That could be exciting. I'll be waiting."

I rang off and waited for Blythe's call back. I didn't have to wait long. In a couple of minutes my phone rang.

"Axe."

"Bliss. I've got what you wanted. That car belongs to a Thaddeus Dumpler. Address, 1304 Packrat Lane. No phone number."

"Dumpler, huh? That's interesting."

"Why interesting?"

"It just is. Thanks, Blythe, I owe you. Tell the kitties hello for me."

I put the receiver in the cradle. So, the kid's name was Dumpler. No doubt the nephew of the dentist. I wondered if Crosby Dumpler had lied to me. Maybe he really was interested in the Ivory Ibis. Maybe he'd conned or bribed his relative into terrorizing Lund, trying to get the treasure map. Tracy and Eben might have been right.

I went outside and started up my car. The Nash was a little cranky. It had grown a lot colder during the night. The sky was overcast. A few snowflakes whirled around in the frozen air. I headed over to Packrat Lane.

10

The Chevy was still parked in front of the house. It was black and even more beat up than I'd realized the night before. I went up onto the porch and pushed the bell button. In a minute a cute little coed answered the door and I asked if I could talk to Thaddeus.

"Ted? I think he's still asleep."

"Get him up. Police business."

"For real? Come in. I'll get him."

I walked into what looked like a communal living room. There was a TV set, some mismatched furniture with the stuffing sticking out, some TV trays with the remains of TV dinners. There was a bookcase stuffed full of textbooks, and a coffee table littered with empty bottles and overflowing ashtrays. Ah, the life of a college student.

Ted came walking into the room a few minutes later. A lad of eighteen or so, with too-long hair greased back above a high forehead. He was wearing jeans and was tucking his shirt in as he came into the room.

"Angie said it was the cops. Who are you, buddy?"

"Axe Hatchett, private investigator. The cops will be here plenty soon if you don't give me the straight dope about what happened last night."

"Huh? Nothing happened last night. Want a beer?"

"No thanks."

"I'm going to get one. I'm a little hung over."

"Make it snappy."

He disappeared a moment, then returned with an opened beer bottle. He sat down in an over-stuffed chair across from mine.

"What's this about?"

"It's about you parking your car in front of Kirsten Lund's house at three o'clock this morning. What were you up to?"

"Who's Christine Lund?"

"Nice try. What were you up to?"

He took a gulp of beer and looked at the ceiling.

"Oh, yeah, now I remember. I didn't stop in front of anyone's house. I mean, not on purpose. See, it was like this. I was driving and smoking a fag. I dropped my smoke and I didn't want it burning a hole in my floor mat."

"Sure, that's a swell ride you've got."

He bristled. "It's what I've got. OK? I dropped my smoke and I stopped the car to look around for it. That's all. What were you doing there?"

"Waiting for you. Let's try again. Why were

you scoping out Dr. Lund's house? If I can't get an honest answer out of you, I'll have to try the old man. You know, Dr. Dumpler."

"Hey, he's my uncle."

"I know."

"Don't go bothering him. I mean, I'm hoping to get some Christmas money out of him. He thinks I'm always in trouble. But he's wrong.

"About last night. Here's the straight dope. Me and a buddy of mine were cruising the streets last night. We had a bottle with us. My buddy, his name is Al, he has this crush on one of our teachers. She's old enough to be his mom, but he likes older chicks. And I got to admit, she ain't bad.

"She's an English prof. Dr. Lund. We were just driving around, like I said, and Al says: 'Hey, that hot Kirsten Lund lives around here. Let's drive by her house.' So I say 'OK.' He told me how to get to her house and I drove there. We stopped out front a minute. That's all."

"Were you hoping to get a peek at her through her bedroom window?"

"No. Her bedroom window is at the back of the house. I mean—that's what Al says. I wouldn't know."

"Of course not. So Al is goofy for Lund? Maybe he should ask her out."

"Sure, buddy, that's a swell idea. Listen, you aren't going to talk about this to my uncle, are you? I didn't do anything wrong. Al's a screwball sometimes."

I stood up.

"I don't know if I believe you. I'm going to tell you this once. Stay away from Lund. You ever hear a story about an ivory ibis?"

"An ivory — ?' He started laughing. "Prof Snelf, yeah. He told us that story in class. Crazy. What about it?"

"You wouldn't be a treasure hunter, would you?"

"Me? Mister, I'm just a student. I pump gas on weekends. I'm only trying to keep my grades decent, and work enough to buy beer. Leave me alone."

"You're too young to buy beer."

"I got some older friends who buy it for me. Nothing wrong with that."

"Keep your nose clean. Where can I find this Al friend of yours? He lives here, doesn't he?"

He set his mouth hard. "I don't rat on my pals."

"What's his full name? Al what?"

"Mister, I don't rat on my pals."

"Maybe your uncle can give me his name. I'll give him a call."

"Do whatever the hell you want."

"OK. You going out of town for the holidays?"

He laughed.

"Sure, I'm flying off to Hawaii. Got some hula girls waiting for me. I got no place to go. Just good old exciting Quartz Quarry."

"You got a phone number where I can reach you?"

"There's a house phone." He gave me the number.

"I'll be watching the Lund place. Me or somebody else."

"You do that. Peeper."

I said a cordial goodbye and left.

Ted was full of it. With or without his uncle's help, he and Al had broken into Kirsten Lund's place and ransacked it. Then, when she came home unexpectedly, they'd tried to scare her into telling them where the treasure map was.

It all fit. It made sense. But I still couldn't figure out why nothing in Lund's apartment had been broken. Ted didn't seem like a big respecter of art. He would have been happy to smash up Lund's carvings. Unless someone told him not to.

I decided not to call Dr. Dumpler at his office. His slick nurse would probably tell me "Doctor" was way too busy to talk to me. I'd try him at home that evening. For the hundredth time

Once again, I regretted having brought along Tracy and Eben to the interview. It wasn't likely that Dumpler would be very cooperative with me now. And speaking of Tracy, I thought I'd drop by Rocko's, smell my girl's dragon breath, and eat a couple of burned burgers with cheese and onions on them.

I cranked up the Nash and headed for the other side of town. As I drove, I started thinking again.

It was just barely possible that Ted and Al were working for Lund, or Umbray, or Crampton. I wished I could get a handle on the case. If murder was in the air, I wanted to swat it down like one of Rocko's flies.

Tracy and Prissy May were fighting when I opened the door. Or, rather, Tracy was yelling while Prissy May smiled happily and nodded her head, and said: "Yes, Tracy," over and over again.

"What's this row about?" I asked. I was the only customer in the place.

"Donuts!" said Tracy. "That's what this row's about. Prissy May's been giving them away."

"I only gave away yesterday's donuts, Tracy."

"In Rocko's, yesterday's donuts are also today's donuts. Sometimes they're even tomorrow's donuts! You know why? Because this is a business, not a charity. Cookie likes to make money. If he starts losing money, then somebody's going to have to get fired."

"It'd be terrible if you got fired, Tracy. I mean, you've been like a mother to me."

"You think it's going to be me who gets canned?"

"Stop it you two," I said. "Why does Cookie let you girls fight like this?"

"He can't hear anything but popping grease back in the kitchen," said Tracy.

"Leave the girl alone. She's only trying to be a good waitress. It's not her fault she ended up at Rocko's. Let me smell your breath."

Tracy stepped closer and breathed all over me.

"Garlic!" I said.

"Yeah, I ate some. I didn't want to offend you with my smoker's breath."

"No more cigarettes, all right?"

"I promise. I haven't smoked since I was a kid. I forgot how much I don't like it. It makes me woozy."

"Like you need that."

"Tracy," said Prissy may, "when are you and Mr. Hatchett tying the knot?" She giggled and clapped her hands. God this girl was chipper.

"New Year's. Day."

"Oh, that's wonderful, if you don't drink. Getting married when you're all hung over wouldn't be much fun."

"What do you know about hangovers?" asked Tracy. "Girls like you don't drink."

"No, but I have an uncle. He stays with us. On Saturday nights he always comes home drunk. And on Sundays he's always cross. Even in church. He swears at the minister."

"I wouldn't mind meeting this uncle of yours," I said.

"OK!"

"How's the case going?" Tracy asked me.

"It's going nowhere. Oh, I've got a lead or two, maybe, and a couple of ideas."

"Tell me."

"Not now. I need to eat."

"When you two get married," Prissy May butted in, "how many kids are you going to have? How long will it be before you're hearing the pitter-patter of little feet?"

I thought of the kittens.

"Axe and me haven't decided if we're going to raise a family."

"Oh, you have to," cried the girl.

"I don't know. Axe is pretty old."

"Thirty-six is not old," I said. "I can't help it if you're only twenty-nine."

"You'd make a swell dad," Tracy said, "but you've said yourself you might not want children."

"I don't want starving children. Business is going to have to pick up before you and me start talking about spawning."

"Things will pick up. And I'll get a swell new job. I promise."

I ate the hamburgers I'd ordered and looked at the clock on the wall.

"It's time I got going," I said, getting off my stool and putting on my hat. Tracy kissed me demurely.

"Do something about that cigar breath," she said.

I tipped my hat at Prissy May and left. Out on the sidewalk I lit a cigar, but when I reached Kirsten Lund's house I ground the cigar butt in the gutter with my shoe. Minnie's car was absent, but the Muntz was still parked out front. There were no other cars near the house. I didn't know what kind of car Kirsten drove, but there was a little garage—about big enough to accommodate a

Model T—at the end of a long drive by the side of the house.

I climbed the porch steps and rang the bell. Lilith answered. She had a bundle of knitting in her arms. A sweater in progress, maybe.

"Come in," she said. "Kirsten and I are getting on each other's nerves. Come in and make us behave."

I came in. Lilith shooed me into a chair. Kirsten was sitting in her wheelchair, near a bed that crowded the living room considerably.

"Welcome," she said. "Is this a professional visit?"

"More or less."

She looked a lot better than she had the night before. She'd obviously been in pain, and she'd had too much punch, but if she was feeling anything but good today, she wasn't showing it.

Lilith sat down on the couch and put her knitting next to her. That's when I saw the gun, Ollie's revolver.

"Sorry," she said. "Kirsten's got me all upset. I'm expecting treasure hunting marauders at any moment."

"I've merely been acquainting her with the facts of my attack."

"Pays to be cautious," I said. "Do either of you know of a student named Ted Dumpler?"

"A magna cum laude in the making," said Lilith.

Kirsten giggled. "He'll be lucky if he's able to

graduate, poor boy. He keeps taking my classes, though I know he hates them."

"Does his friend Al attend those classes?"

"Al Marbels? Yes, the two are inseparable. Why do you ask about them?"

"Because they dropped by for a visit last night. They parked in front of your house, with their headlights dimmed, for about five minutes. Any idea why?"

Kirsten lost her smile and made an uncomfortable sound in her throat. "How do you know about this?" she asked.

"I was parked across the street, keeping an eye on your place. Sorry, it's part of my job."

"So Eben hired you?"

"Yes."

"I can take care of myself."

"Clearly," I said, staring pointedly at her cast.

"Why would those boys do something like that?" Lilith asked Kirsten, who shrugged.

"Little Al's in love with me. He practically drools in class."

"I thought he did that with every female," said Lilith. "He's that way in my classes, too."

"He clearly needs a girlfriend," I said.

"Good luck to him."

"Did you tell the police about this?" Kirsten asked me.

"No. The cops are on their own. This is my case."

"Do you think they had anything to do with

my — accident?"

"Maybe," I said. "Ted's got an uncle who's an amateur treasure hunter. He's had some success. Maybe the uncle told Ted about the ivory ibis. I know Dr. Snelf did."

"You know a lot," said Lilith, without sarcasm. Her face looked a bit strained, and her smile had disappeared.

"I try to do my job."

"Lilith, keep that gun close by," said Kirsten.

"Don't worry. What are we supposed to do, Mr. Hatchett?"

"Axe. Well, you can tell the cops if you want. Or you can trust me to keep you safe. But don't count on me too much. I wish there was a way we could prove to these guys that there's no treasure map."

"Kirsten, are you sure you don't want Ollie to stay with us?" asked Lilith. "Of course, I don't know where he'd sleep. We're pretty crowded here."

"That's up to you, honey. I don't think he'd be sleeping with Minnie, so he'd have to bunk with you upstairs."

"He wouldn't be sleeping with me," said Lilith, with some heat.

"If you say so. The house is crowded enough with just three of us. A fourth would be impossible. We'll be OK. Do you have an extra gun I could borrow, Mr. Hatchett — Axe?"

"I'm not big on loaning out my guns, but I

could probably find one for you. Do you know how to shoot?"

"I've seen it done in the movies."

"Sure. They make it look easy. The best thing that can happen is for me to get to the bottom of things."

"Can you get Al and Ted arrested?" asked Kirsten.

"Can you prove it was them who attacked you?"

"No. And I'm really not sure it was them. The two men who broke into my house sounded older. Men, not boys. But I'm not really clear about anything that happened that night. You'd think it'd be burned into my memory, but that's not how it is."

"Understandable enough. I'll be continuing my nightly vigils, but I likely won't be available during the day. Be careful who you let into this house. And if anything comes up you think I should know about, give me a call. I'll give you three numbers where you might be able to reach me. And a fourth number for Christmas day, if this thing lasts that long."

"We'll be careful, and we'll keep in touch," said Lilith. "Thanks for your help."

"He's getting paid for it," said Kirsten. She seemed angry all of a sudden. I wondered why.

It didn't look like I was going to get anything else out of the interview, so I bid my adieus to the ladies and departed.

11

Like a sap, I'd forgotten to switch cars with Tracy — again — when I'd gone to Rocko's. I headed back to the diner. When I got there, Tracy was alone at the counter.

"Tell me you didn't kill her," I said.

"I wish. No, she's doing some last minute Christmas shopping. Cookie gave her the rest of the day off."

"That must make you happy."

"I know she's a nice kid, but, jeez, she's driving me nuts."

"You didn't have a long way to go. Listen, can I switch cars with you for a couple of days?"

"Are you going to tell me all you've learned about the case?"

I told her the little I knew.

"Dentist Dumpler's nephew, huh? I bet he's a born killer, too. That kind of thing runs in families."

"If you say so."

"Why don't you drag him and his chum down to the police station?"

"I've got nothing on them. They could both be completely innocent."

"What about what happened last night?"

"Ted might have been telling me the truth. Al has a crush on Kirsten and wanted to drive by her house. If that's all there was to it, it's hardly a federal crime."

"Hurry up and solve this case, will you? I don't want you spoiling our Christmas."

"You know, I've been thinking. Instead of going to your folks, wouldn't it be fun for us to cook our own little Christmas dinner? Just the two of us?"

"We'd get food poisoning. You don't know how to cook, and all I know is what Cookie taught me, which ain't much."

"Why didn't your folks teach you how to cook when you were growing up?"

"I don't know. You can ask them when we go to their place for Christmas dinner."

"All right, I give up."

"Good. You can borrow my car. But don't stink it up with cigar smoke."

"Yes, ma'am."

Tracy kept her car parked in the alley behind Rocko's. I left my Nash in its place and drove over to my office. I wanted to pick up my camera, a big flashlight, and a second gun. I keep my guns at home, but I have one in the office that I took off a mean drunk in an alley a year or so ago. I should have turned it over to the cops, but I didn't. I thought maybe I'd loan it to Kirsten after giving her some brief shooting instructions.

There were no notes pinned to my office door, but when I went inside I saw an envelope that somebody had shoved under my door. I pulled a scrap of paper out of it. The note read: "Axe, having a hard time getting ahold of you. Me and Celeste and the baby are on our way to Texas for Christmas. Be back the 28th Have a merry Christmas. Bram."

So that's where the deserter went.

I gathered up the camera and the flashlight, and took the old revolver from my desk drawer. It was a nickel-plated Iver Johnson. It was only a thirty-two, but that's better than nothing. I put it in my coat pocket. Before I left, I called the Lund place. Minnie answered.

"Where you been?" I asked.

"Running errands. Who is this?"

"Axe Hatchett."

"Oh, hello. Did you wish to speak to Dr. Lund?"

"No. Just tell her I'm bringing over a little gift."

"How nice. She'll like that."

"I think she will. I'll be over in a little while."

"All right. We'll be here. How's the case coming along?"

"I've had headaches I liked better."

I got in Tracy's jalopy and drove to Lund's again. The snow was really coming down now. I hoped we weren't in for another blizzard like the one we'd had a month earlier. The roads were a little slick and I fish-tailed some as I drove. Minnie's Dodge was parked out front, but Lilith's nice little Muntz was absent. I wondered what kind of money she was making to afford such a sweet boat.

Minnie opened the door before I could even ring the bell.

"How are you, Mr. Hatchett? We were just having some tea. Would you like some?"

"No thanks. I'm not staying."

I walked back into the living room. Kirsten was in bed, reading a book. She was wearing black pajamas that looked good with her skin. She'd had to slit one pajama leg to accommodate the cast. I pulled the little revolver out of my pocket and handed it to her butt first. She grasped it enthusiastically.

"Just line up the sights and squeeze the trigger," I told her. "There's six rounds in the cylinder. If that's not enough, you're out of luck."

"If those hired thugs return, I'll be ready for them."

"Great. Where's Dr. Umbray?"

"She went over to Ollie's to pick up some more of her things."

"That's a swell little sports car she's got. You professors must do pretty well for yourselves."

Kirsten snorted. "I wish that were true." she said. "The car was a gift. Lilith's people have money."

"Somebody has to, I guess. All's quiet on the home front?"

"Quiet to the point of dullness. I wish I could go out."

"You're better off resting up. That leg has to be bothering you."

"It hurts some. That means it's healing."

"Dr. Lund told me about those awful boys who came around last night," said Minnie. "Thank goodness you were there to protect us."

"They didn't even see me. I doubt if they'll be back. I had a talk with one of them. A nice boy named Ted."

"Ted Dumpler and Al Marbels. They're trouble. I'm sure they're the ones who broke Dr. Lund's leg."

"I'm not sure of that at all, but I'm going to find out. I'll leave you ladies to your tea. I just wanted to drop off the gun."

"Thank you," said Kirsten.

"I'm afraid of guns myself," said Minnie. "Don't bring me one."

"How about a machete?"

"I've been keeping a rolling pin under my pillow."

"Thanks for telling me. I won't try to break into the place. I'll be in the neighborhood again tonight. In fact, I ought to head home for a nap. Good bye."

I drove home. Kirsten had said something interesting. She had said that if those hired thugs returned, she'd be ready for them. How did she know they were hired? Why couldn't they be working on their own? The comment might not have meant much, but it set off a tiny alarm in my skull. Sometimes the little things end up mattering.

I did take a nap when I got home. Then I fixed and ate an unappetizing dinner. Tracy had been right; if we cooked our own Christmas dinner it would probably be our last meal ever. At six I called Dumpler at his home. His wife, I presume, answered. I asked to speak to Crosby and she didn't ask who was calling.

"Good evening?" said Dumpler.

"It's me, Axe Hatchett."

"Oh, it's you. How are your ill-mannered operatives?"

"They're no longer in my employ. I apologize for their behavior, but they had good references. Listen, I wanted to talk to you about your nephew, Ted."

"Talk to his parents. I suppose the boy's in trouble again."

"Not necessarily. But he was prowling around in the neighborhood of the woman who was attacked the other night by treasure hunters. You know, the ivory ibis incident."

"You think I put him up to it? I told you I have no interest in that ridiculous story. And I certainly wouldn't do anything illegal in the course of searching for lost treasure, no matter what your associates think."

"But maybe you put the idea into his head. Did you tell him about the ivory ibis?"

"I rarely speak to the boy. No, I told him nothing about any ivory ibis. No doubt he heard the story from someone at the college. Now, if you'll excuse me, my wife's putting our dinner on the table."

He hung up. I had learned absolutely nothing. I wondered if I could somehow set up a trap. I had the ivory ibis that Kirsten had carved for herself. Was there any way I could use it as bait to catch a treasure hunter, or a possible would-be murderer? I'd have to think about it. There was nothing for me to do now but wait until it got good and dark and then resume my stakeout.

I kept thinking about that damned carved bird. I looked out my window to see if Blythe Bliss was home. Her car was in the yard behind her cottage. I paid her a visit.

"You again?" Blythe said, when she'd opened the door for me. "Can't get enough of those kittens, huh?"

"They're cute little shavers, but actually I'm here to borrow that bird I gave you."

"I thought it was your little gift to me.."

"Sorry. I never gave it to you. You'll have to carve your own."

"Wait here, I'll fetch it." She disappeared and showed up again a minute later. She handed me the box.

"Where you been keeping it?"

"None of your business. If they torture you to get it, you won't have to worry about spilling your guts to them."

"That's reassuring. Thanks."

"My pleasure. What are you going to do with it?"

"I don't know yet. I've got a half-baked idea kicking around in my brain, that's all. I thought I might need the bird. Tell my kittens their dad asked after them."

"You're one of those dads that are always working, never have time for their children."

"That's me. I'll talk to you later."

"Bye."

I put the dingus in its box in the trunk of the Chevy. It wasn't dark out yet, but I started up the car and took off down the road anyway. Sometimes driving helps me think. Without really knowing what I was doing, I ended up in front of Ollie Crampton's house. Lilith's robin's-egg-blue Muntz was nowhere in sight. Neither was Crampton's silver-and-red Willys, but there was a little garage in back of the house, like Kirsten's, and the station wagon could have been parked there.

I got out, opened the Chevy's trunk, and collected the bird box. Then I strolled carelessly up the front walk and rang the doorbell. No answer. I leaned on the bell button again. Still no answer. I walked around to the back and pounded on the back door. Silence. Good. That's what I wanted.

Taking a couple of lock picks out of my wallet, I went to work on the back door lock. It was an old lock and gave me no trouble at all. I walked through a kitchen, a tiny dining room, and into the living room where Lilith had received me and Eben earlier.

I took the ivory ibis out of its box and cleared a space on the mantel for it, trying not to rearrange any dust. Then I went back out the back door and locked it.

It was full dark by this time, so I drove straight over to Kirsten's. I sat in Tracy's car and contemplated my sins.

12

I had no idea what my practical joke with the ivory ibis would bring about. Maybe nothing. Maybe panic, anger, or confusion. Sometimes you just have to try things. I had another idea of a joke I could play, but I would have to wait until tomorrow to put it into effect, if at all.

The Willys, the Muntz, and the Dodge were all in their spots. Lights were on in the downstairs only. I hoped everyone was having a good time. I wasn't.

I was well rested, and that went against me. If I'd been a little tired I wouldn't have been so fidgety. I played the radio for a time. It was still plenty early to pick up stations. But there was nothing on but Christmas music, and I was already tired of that.

For a while I tuned into a radio drama, but I got bored with all the breathless tragedy and switched it off. It was going to be a long night.

The snow kept falling and piling up. I had to

use my windshield wipers a few times to keep the windshield clear of snow. I didn't really expect Ted and Al to show up, but I was disappointed when they didn't.

Around ten, Ollie came out of the house and drove off in his car. About twelve, some lights went on upstairs and the lights downstairs went out. I waited, and waited. A little after midnight the front door opened slowly and Lilith appeared. She took off quietly in the Muntz. Visiting the archaeologist, no doubt. At least she and Ollie were going to have some fun. I wondered if Kirsten would notice Lilith's absence. That could spell trouble of a green-eyed variety.

Dawn finally came, as it always does. Lilith returned and crept into the house. I stayed where I was for another hour and then drove home. The old Chevy started right up. When I got home, my headlights lit-up a mournful sight. My half-wild skunk, Ambrosia, was sitting in the snow with an accusatory look on her face. She wanted bacon, and I had failed to provide it.

I hurried inside, fried up a couple of slices, and brought them outside. Ambrosia was still waiting. She took the bacon from my hand and then disappeared under the house. The things some people have to do to get a bite to eat. I hit the sack and slept like the living dead.

I got up around eleven. I couldn't wait to get out, and so I skipped my morning coffee and eggs. I drove over to what we call Lesser Downtown, an area with an unsavory reputation. There were a couple of pawnshops I wanted to visit. The owners were none too particular about the temperature of customer's pledges. A number of stolen items made their way into both shops. I figured whoever had filched the original ivory ibis, from the museum, may have wanted to make a bad situation a little better by trying to sell the thing. A few bucks cash was no substitute for a tomb full of gold artifacts, but at least it was something.

The first shop I visited was owned by a former sailor with lots of tattoos and beefy muscles. He looked at me cross-eyed when I walked in. But he couldn't help it. He'd been born cross-eyed. How he'd ever talked his way into the Navy I'll never know.

"Help you?" he asked. Pawn shop proprietors and bartenders are similarly laconic.

"I'm looking for a figurine. A bird. Or, actually, a man with a bird's head. Ivory, with some black and gold designs on it. About yay high." I showed him with my hands.

"So?"

"Do you have anything like that?"

"Look around."

What a guy. I looked around. I didn't see any ivory ibises.

"Did you sell it already?'

"I ain't sold no ivory bird."

"The owner really wants it back. Her nephew stole it and pawned it without her knowing it.

She's a sweet little old grandmother."

"Is she?"

"Yeah. Did you sell the bird or not?"

"I couldn't have sold it. It was never in this shop."

"Why didn't you tell me that in the first place?"

"I thought maybe you'd see something you liked. Just trying to make a living."

"Try making it without me." I left.

The second shop was only a couple of blocks from the other one, so I walked.

This place was owned by a German with a beer gut and gaps in his teeth. He smiled big when I came in.

"Help you, can I?"

"I hope so. You know what an ibis is?"

"A board game? Like the dominoes?"

"No. A bird. Egyptian. I'm looking for a statue, no more than a foot high. It's carved out of ivory. There's black and gold designs on it."

"This is a real bird? I have two canaries. Good singers. You want I should make them sing?" He pulled a blackjack out from under the counter.

"No, leave them alone. The bird I'm looking for isn't alive. It's as dead as Moses. It's a statue, a figurine. It's a guy's body but with a bird's head. The head has a long beak. My niece stole it from me and I want it back. I'm willing to pay for it, and I don't want to have to go to the police."

"I don't want you should go to the cops either. A bird. How much money you think you pay?"

"Show me the bird first."

"No cops? For sure?"

"I don't even like cops. Show me the bird."

He got off his stool, came around from behind the counter, and disappeared amidst his inventory. In a couple of minutes he came back, holding a big chicken made of wood.

"That's a chicken," I said. "I'm looking for an ibis. Egyptian bird with a long beak. It's got a man's body."

"Oh, an ibis. Not a chicken?"

I shook my head. He went back into the depths of his shop. In a minute he came back carrying something else. It was the ivory carving of a man with a bird's head. The head had a long beak.

"That's it!" I said. "How much?"

"For something so beautiful as this? Twenty bucks."

"You're nuts. Five bucks."

"For that I couldn't let you touch it. Twenty."

"I'm telling you, my niece stole it from me. To buy hash."

"Hash. Tender roast beef, carrots and some potatoes. Some onion."

"No."

"No onion?"

"Not that kind of hash. The kind you smoke."

"I say twenty dollars."

"I'll call the cops. You're trying to sell me stolen goods."

"When your cops they should get here, I don't

think this most beautiful bird they will find."

"You're a crook. Ten bucks."

"Yes, for you. Ten bucks."

Damned Kraut. I paid the louse and walked off with my prize. I found a pay phone and made two calls. I dialed the house number Ted had given me. A girl answered, maybe the same Angie who had let me into Ted's house. I asked for Al and was told he was out. Did I want to leave a message? I told her no, that. I'd call back later. No doubt Ted had warned Al about me and told him to be a good little boy and not talk to strangers. But it was worth a try. Next, I called Tracy at Rocko's.

"Rocko's! Yeah?"

"Tracy, my little gooseberry tart, It's your dreamboat. Is there any chance you could take off work for an hour or so?"

"I'd love it. Cookie won't care. He'll still have his little Prissy May."

"Great. Do you have an old grocery sack around there, maybe in the kitchen? And some string?"

"Probably. Are you getting ready to wrap my Christmas present?"

"No, somebody else's."

"It's not for one of those dames you're working for, is it?"

"I'm working for Eben. I'll be by in ten minutes. OK?"

"You're not at home?"

"No. I'm working. Get some eggs and bacon started for me, will you? And make some fresh coffee."

"Sure, cabbage roll. See you in a bit. I'll check on the paper bag."

Rocko's was also in Lesser Downtown. I was there in a few minutes.

When I walked into the grease-drenched diner, Prissy May was cooing over a customer, a big guy in coveralls, and Tracy was watching the interaction with clear disapproval. She stuck her head into the hole in the wall between the kitchen and the counter and came away with a plate of eggs and bacon for yours truly.

"Eat up. I'll get your coffee." She filled a crockery mug until it overflowed, a trick she never tired of playing on me.

"Let's see the present you're giving to some lucky twist."

I pulled the ibis out of my overcoat pocket and presented it to her. She cooed, and ooed and ahed.

"It's beautiful. Is this the one the Lund frail gave you?"

"No. This is the one that was stolen from the college museum."

"How'd you end up with it?"

"I liberated it from a pawn shop."

"And who are you giving it to?"

"Kirsten Lund and Lilith Umbray. They'll have to share it."

"What kind of crazy business is that? What are

you up to, Axe?"

"I'm trying to stir the pot a little. Could be nothing will come of it. I'm going to wrap it up in this grocery sack paper and you're going to deliver it for me."

"I get to drive."

"Sure, it's your car." Tracy hadn't driven much in the years before she bought her jalopy and she needed the practice.

The guy in the coveralls finished his meal, paid for it, then winked at the cute counter girl and left. Prissy May turned my way and turned on a smile that almost burned my retinas.

"Hi, Mr. Hatchett."

"Hi yourself."

I took out my jack knife and cut the grocery bag into wide strips. Then I rolled the ibis up in one strip and tied off the ends with some string. It looked like a giant Tootsie Roll.

"Elegant," said Tracy.

"Wait until you see your present."

"I can hardly wait."

"You ready? Let's get going."

Tracy gave Prissy May some instructions, laced with threats, and we headed out. Tracy readjusted the Chevy's seat to accommodate her limited stature, and I gave her directions to Lund's place.

"What's supposed to happen when Lund, or whoever, opens this parcel?"

"I don't know. But I hope something happens. When we get there I'll have you park about a block away. Walk down to Lund's, I'll give you the house number. Try sneaking up onto the porch. Ring the bell and leave the package on the doorstep. Then high-tail it out of there and come back to me. If anybody sees you and stops you don't tell them anything. Just say somebody gave you a buck to drop off the package. And refuse to describe the person."

"Who would I describe? You?"

"Just clam up."

We reached Lund's neighborhood, parked, and Tracy went into action. As she walked down the sidewalk she kept looking around, even over her shoulder, like she thought an army must be following her. It was going to take a while to turn her into a decent operative.

The snow had stopped during the night. It was cold, but the sky was clear. The slush along the gutters was dirty with car exhaust and muddy feet. The bare trees looked brittle and frail. I was too far away to see Kirsten's house. It seemed to take Tracy forever to carry out her mission, but I finally saw her returning, practically running. She was breathless when she got back in the car.

"I did it. But that Lund dame saw me out the window when I went up on the porch. She opened the door as soon as I rang the bell. She moves pretty fast for a lady in a wheelchair. I just handed her the package. She asked me some questions but I pretended I was a deaf mute and took off as fast as I could. You didn't tell me she was such a looker."

"She's all right, I guess."

"She looks like a lady Viking. That hair! What does the other one look like? That Lilith creature?"

"She makes Lund look like an Egyptian mummy."

"Huh? That better not be true, or I'm pulling you off this case right now."

"You aren't my boss, yet. Thanks for your help, by the way."

"It was a pleasure. Now I've got to go back to Prissy May."

"Try getting along with her, why don't you?"

"I can't. We're too different."

"I don't think you're so different. You're both swell kids. Cookie's ruined you, that's all. I'll bet that when you were first working at Rocko's you were all smiles and politeness. Am I right?"

"I can't remember. Maybe. The truth is, I wish I was like Prissy May now. She makes me feel like a heel, but I'm really afraid she'll get fired if I don't help toughen her up."

"Let her get fired. She'll find another job. She'll be better off."

"Then what happens to Cookie? Nobody in their right mind would want to work for him."

Tracy was driving. I looked over at her. She was practically crying. What the hell?

"Listen," I said, "Cookie's not your lookout. He's a grown man. Let him take care of himself."

"I've been with him for three years. He's not a bad guy, just a bad cook."

"Maybe he can give-up slinging poison hash and start a bar or something. He'll be OK. We need to find a new place for you to work."

"And poor Prissy May?"

"We'll find something for her, too. Quit worrying."

"I'll try."

Tracy drove us back to Rocko's. She got out and I slid over into the driver's seat and put it back where it belonged. She was still standing by the driver's door. I cranked down the window and she gave me a quick kiss.

"You did swell, kid," I told her.

"Thanks, Chief. Let me know when the fireworks start going off."

I drove home and flopped in bed again. I sincerely hoped the phone would wake me up and it'd be Lund, or somebody, telling me about the reappearing ibises. But when the phone finally did ring, an hour later, it was Eben.

"I hope I haven't awakened you," he said. "There have been a couple of new developments."

"Oh?" I asked, innocently.

"Yes. The ibises have come back to Capistrano, so to speak."

"Meaning?"

"You remember when we were over at Dr. Crampton's? You and I and Lilith attempted to find the copy of the ivory ibis that Kirsten had carved for him. Lilith said it had been resting on the mantel."

"Sure. And we couldn't find it. What about it?"

"Ollie stumbled across it this morning. It was on the mantel. He said he'd noticed footprints in the snow around his house last night. Someone had come up to the porch then gone around to the back door. He said there were slushy footprints on his kitchen linoleum. Some intruder, probably the same one who stole the ibis in the first place, picked the lock on the backdoor and returned the figure."

"Some lowlife bum. Crazy, too, if you ask me."

"Doubtless. And then early this afternoon, Kirsten had a visitor. A short young woman, possibly deaf and dumb, and with the look of insanity in her eyes, delivered a plain brown parcel. Guess what was in it?"

"A fruitcake? A pony?"

"Stop being frivolous. The ivory ibis stolen from our little museum."

"That's impossible. This must be some kind of joke. What sick, twisted, hooligan would do such a thing? What can it possibly mean?"

"Kirsten thinks it might be a warning of some sort. The thieves are perhaps reminding Kirsten and Lilith of their presence. It appears quite ominous to me."

"Was Lund pretty upset?"

"Unspeakably. I talked to her on the phone. I've never known her to sound so frantic."

"That's a shame. So, what do you want me to do about it?"

"I don't know, you're the detective. I might advise you to visit Kirsten, see if you can calm her down."

"How did Ollie react to his break-in, and the return of his bird?"

"I haven't talked to him, or Lilith. Perhaps you can talk to them."

"I can try. Listen, thanks for the information."

"I hope it will prove useful."

"So do I. I'll give Lund a call a little later."

"Thank you. Keep in touch."

We hung up. I dialed the number for Ted and Al's house again. A guy answered.

"Yeah?"

"Can I speak to Al Marbels?"

"You're talking to him."

"Oh, how's it going, Al?"

"Who is this?"

"A well-wisher. Say, Kirsten Lund is a friend of mine. I hear you're interested in showing her a good time. I might be able to help with that."

"Who are you? Some kind of kidder? Are you that flatfoot Ted talked to?"

"I'm no flatfoot, just an honest sleuth."

"You go to hell, pal. And tell that bitch to leave me alone, her and her crazy goddamned plans. It's the bunk."

He slammed down the phone hard enough to make my ears ring. And I was so looking forward to a nice long chat. What had he meant about Kirsten's crazy plans? Had she really hired Ted and Al to break into her house? Interesting. I gave Lund a call and invited myself over. She didn't sound very warm and cordial, but she didn't try to keep me away, either. I fired up Tracy's ride and ferried over.

When I got to the front door I could hear voices inside. I was about to punch the doorbell button when the voices went up in pitch. Angry female voices. I thought the door would be locked but it wasn't. I pushed my way in, then opened the second door that led to Minnie's apartment.

A surprise awaited me. Kirsten was sitting in her wheelchair, leveling the little Iver Johnson I'd loaned her at Lilith, who was standing at the other end of the room, Ollie's forty-four aimed at Kirsten. Other people with guns make me nervous. I pulled my Chief's Special, though I didn't aim it at anyone.

"I hope I'm not intruding," I said, the sarcasm dripping from my slack jaws.

The two women deflated and lowered their guns.

"It's all right," said Kirsten, with surprising calm. "Lilith and I were just discussing next semester's curriculum."

"You two must take that stuff pretty seriously."

"Actually," said Lilith, "we were acting like a couple of bratty children with guns. Kirsten and I don't always get along. Our enforced chumminess is getting to both of us."

"Maybe I should round up the side arms."

"Don't," said Kirsten, "We might need them. And not for each other. Do you see what's on Minnie's coffee table?"

The coffee table had been pushed into a corner to make room for the bed. The ivory ibis was sitting on it. I went over and looked at it like I'd never seen it before.

"Nice," I said. "Did you carve a new one?"

"Do you really think I could climb up to my workshop to do any carving?"

"Where'd it come from, then?"

"It's the original, the one taken from our illustrious museum. A girl—kind of pretty, but crazy-looking—delivered it today. I couldn't get a word out of her."

Pretty? I didn't know Tracy was pretty. And Eben had claimed she was charming. I'd have to take another look at my best girl.

"What kind of monkey business is this? Why would the thief return the ibis, and to you?"

"Tell him the rest, Lilith."

Lilith turned my way, put the big revolver down on an end table.

"Remember the ibis statue we couldn't find at Ollie's? I mean, Dr. Crampton's?" She gave Kirsten a dark look.

"Sure. We couldn't find it. You said it had been on Ollie's fireplace mantel."

"That's right, and that's where it was this morning."

"Huh?"

"It's reappeared. Whoever stole it brought it back while the house was empty. They broke in and left the ibis and didn't take anything else."

"That's impossible. Why would the treasure hunters do that?"

Kirsten shrugged. "If the third one shows up I'm going to scream."

"It can't. I've got it. It's in a safe place."

"Kirsten thinks her attackers are trying to scare her, and maybe me."

"It's working," said Lund.

"That reminds me, Dr. Lund," I said. "I have a message to pass onto you, though it's a bit profane."

Kirsten raised her eyebrows.

What's the message?"

"Well, I had a brief conversation with Al Marbels. He said to tell you to leave him alone. You and your God-damned crazy plans. Can you make heads or tails of that?"

Lund was prettily made up today, and dressed nicely. Lilith was in a similar state of beauty. Were they throwing their looks at each other? Kirsten's face was too heavily powdered to show any change of color, but her throat reddened and then paled as I watched for her reaction to the message I'd passed on.

"I'll talk to the President about getting Al expelled. How dare he? And what could he have possibly been talking about? Does the little idiot think I reciprocate his feelings?"

It was my turn to shrug. I did. "Have you talked to the cops lately?"

"No," said Kirsten. "They irritate me."

"Gee, I hope I don't irritate you," I said. "I'm only trying to help."

"Then get to the bottom of this frightful mess. Don't waste Eben's money."

"I'm doing everything I can. If I talk to Al again, is there anything you'd like me to say to him?"

Kirsten gave me a look that would have bored holes through a bank vault.

"I have nothing to say to Al, thank you,"

"Maybe it was Al and Ted who attacked you," suggested Lilith.

"You're just getting around to thinking of that?" asked Kirsten.

"Maybe I don't dwell on the situation like you do."

I was beginning to feel slightly unwanted. These dames wanted to get back to their fighting. I stood up.

"I think I'll be going," I said. "I'll think about this returning ibis business and see what I can come up with."

"Thanks for stopping by," said Kirsten.

"My pleasure. Don't fight any duels, you two."

Lilith laughed. "We'll behave like proper young ladies," she said.

I said my goodbyes and left. I dropped by my office for a minute. There were no notes pinned to my door, nor were there any messages on my office floor. I went home, stopping on the way for a quick meal at an automat.

13

What was I to think of the behavior of Kirsten and Lilith? Would they have actually shot each other if I hadn't come along? And what of Lund's reaction to my message from Al? Was she merely offended at the pipsqueak's romantic fantasies, or was it something else?

Kirsten, at least, had been obviously upset by the reappearing ibises, but who in her situation wouldn't have been? I wanted to get a chance to talk to Ollie again. Maybe I'd give him a call. In fact, right now seemed a good time. I looked up his home number in the phone book and dialed it. It rang seven times before he picked up.

"In the shower!" he practically shouted into the phone. "I hope this is important."

"Sorry, I didn't mean to disturb you. This is Axe Hatchett. I'll let you get back to your shower in a minute. I just have a couple of questions."

"Sure, I didn't mean to growl at you. What's on your mind?"

"I talked to Kirsten. She said a couple of those figurines, those ibises, showed up."

"Damned strange, isn't it? What kind of jokers are we dealing with here?"

"You got me. Somebody went to some trouble to have those birds return to the coop. What do you think it means?"

"I'm damned if I know. Kirsten thinks it's some kind of warning from the treasure hunters, and I think she might be right. You got any other ideas?"

"Not a one."

"Look, are you going to be guarding Kirsten and Lilith's house tonight?"

"I'll be there, from a little after dark until a little after sunrise."

"Happy to hear it. Where will you be parked?"

"Well, about half a block down from the house. I'll be able to see the front of the house and part of one side. That's the best I can do."

"Which side?"

"Does it matter? The side the living room's on."

"That's good, because that's likely where they'll be most of the time. Thanks for your help."

"I'm getting paid for it."

"Say, the girl profs told me about those college kids hanging around Kirsten's house. Have you looked into that?"

"I'm working on it."

"I think maybe those two are behind the whole thing. I believe they attacked Kirs."

"You could be right. Listen, I'll let you get back to your shower."

"Thanks. Keep me informed, will you?"

"I will."

We said our goodbyes and hung up. Like a vampire, I waited for the sun to go down. There wasn't much I could do while I waited except think. I was getting kind of tired of thinking. I wondered why Ollie was so interested in where I was going to park while I watched Lund's house? What was it to him? Was he just making sure I kept a proper eye on his former lover, or did he have something planned he didn't want me to know about?

When it got good and dark, I stirred the Chevy to life and drove over to my stakeout post. Minnie's and Lilith's cars were parked out front, and an hour later Ollie's Willys showed up. He stayed a couple of hours and then left.

Around midnight I was beginning to nod off. Nothing on the radio. A few snow showers had showed up, and I entertained myself by turning the wipers on and off.

The girls were still up. The living room windows were still lit up. The curtains were thin and I could see Kirsten's silhouette passing back and forth in front of one of the windows. She was in her wheelchair, obviously, and she looked like a child or a midget walking back and forth. I wondered if she and Lilith were arguing again.

At ten minutes after midnight, the window

shattered. I saw glass fall. A split second later a gunshot boomed through the neighborhood.

I was out of my car in a hurry. I ran toward the house. At first I'd figured Lilith had shot Kirsten, but the shot had been too loud. It came from a rifle, and from outside.

I jumped up onto the porch and tried the door. The damned thing was locked. I pounded on it and shouted. Nothing happened, but somebody screamed inside.

I hit the door with my shoulder, hard. I hit it again. Wood split around the frame and the door gave. I pushed my way in.

Lilith was standing in the living room. She held Ollie's revolver and she gave me a look of pure, unadulterated, fear. Kirsten's wheel chair had fallen over and her body was sprawled on the floor. I noticed the cast on her leg had split open. There was blood on it, and on the floor, and on Kirsten.

I stepped up close to her. Under her fanned-out hair I could see that most of her head was gone. Broken like a pumpkin. Lilith was screaming, but I hardly heard her. I turned and shouted at her to call the cops and to keep that revolver close.

"I—I. She — " She couldn't talk.

"Do what I said. I'm going outside."

She screamed again. I headed out the door and around the side of the house.

There were footprints in the snow but I couldn't see them well in the curtained light from the window. No more screams were coming from the house. I ran across the street and down the block to my car. I grabbed my flashlight from the seat. There were lights in windows all up and down the block, windows that had been dark only minutes before. There were even a few muffled figures out in their yards. Somebody yelled; "Hey, you!" I ignored them and ran back across the street.

The snow was coming down harder now. When I found the footprints again — they'd been made by pretty big shoes — they were already filling up with snow. They ended about ten feet from the window, along the side of the house.

I followed them the other direction. They went all along the side of the house and into the alley. I kept following them. After about half a block, they ended. Then fresh car tracks appeared. The killer had parked here.

He'd walked to Kirsten's house, shot her through the curtained window, at the silhouette of her slowly-moving figure. A risky shot, but fatal. It also meant he hadn't gone close enough to the window for the street light to shine on him. After he'd killed Dr. Lund he'd backtracked, walked down the alley, gone to his car and driven away.

He'd been carrying a rifle. If anybody had happened to look out a back window they might have seen him, though the alley was pretty dark. You don't just walk down an alley with a rifle in your hands, especially not right after you've fired the damned thing. How did he conceal it? It could have been a short-barreled rifle, a carbine. He could have held it down by his side, with the barrel along his leg, the stock tucked under his armpit. If he'd been wearing an overcoat, that gun might not have been that noticeable. And the alley was pretty dark, lit up only by a few back porch lights.

I followed the tire tracks until I got to the cross street. There was no point in my following them any farther. I returned to the house. Before I got there I heard a siren. Damn! The police were already there. There was no possibility they'd let me back into the house, and they might detain me. I was sure they wouldn't let me talk to Lilith. I made my way to the front porch. I started up the steps but a big cop stood in the open doorway.

"Shove off, bub!" he said. "There's nothing to see here. Some punk set off a firecracker, that's all."

"I'm a witness. I heard the shot. I was the first one in the house after Dr. Lund was murdered."

"That so?"

"Yeah. There's a woman in there. She's hysterical. She needs somebody's help."

"She'll be OK. We're taking care of her. We'll take her to the hospital. Come up on the porch."

I went up on the porch.

"You live around here?"

"No. I'm a private investigator. I was watching the Lund house."

"What for?"

"Don't you know? Dr. Lund was attacked a

couple of days ago. I was hired to look out for her."

"You did a good job, didn't you?"

"Rub it in, flatfoot." I took a step forward. I swear I would have hit the guy, but just then another officer came to the door. At the same time, a siren switched off behind me. I turned my head. A second squad car had arrived. And I heard a third siren getting louder as it approached. That was likely an ambulance.

"Who you jawing with out here, Donaldson?"

"A shamus. Claims he's a witness."

The second officer pushed the first one out of the way and stood facing me.

"That right, mister?"

"Sure. I was across the street when the shot was fired. I was on stakeout. I was trying to protect Dr. Lund, the dead woman."

"That's tough. I'm sorry. I'm Captain Liverall."

"Axe Hatchett, private dick."

"Tell me what you saw."

I told him, and a lot of other things. He kept me on the porch a long time. Long enough to watch Lilith leave the house, guarded by a third cop, and be led to one of the squad cars. Long enough to see a guy with a pipe and a slouch hat show up. A guy I recognized as the town's coroner. And then they finally let me go, with a warning to stay in town and be ready to answer more questions. Like I was the killer! Sometimes I can't stand cops.

I'd told them about Ted and Al and given them

the phone number of their home, and the address. I even gave them Ted Dumpler's car's license number, though they should have already had it.

When I was a free man again, I went back to the Chevy and drove it to a pay phone. I called Eben. He answered on the fourth ring.

"Hello? Mulford residence."

"Eben, it's Axe." I didn't say anything more, and Eben was silent for several seconds.

"Axe, has something happened?"

"I'll say. I'm sorry. I've let you down. I've let you down as badly as one friend can let down another."

More silence, then: "It's Kirsten, isn't it? She's — is she?"

"She's been shot. I'm sorry to say she's dead."

"Good lord! Good lord! Heavens. How can that be? Her leg's in a cast, she — "

"Somebody shot her through her living room window, with a rifle. I'll get whoever it was, I promise you, if you can believe me."

Another long silence.

"Axe, old man. Don't blame yourself. You were doing your job. You're a good detective, but you can't figure out everything. No one can. Don't be hard on yourself."

"Would it be all right if I came over and saw you?"

"Please do. Please do."

I hung up. I called Tracy. The phone rang forever, and then she picked up.

"Axe?"

"How'd you know it was me?"

"Who else would call me at this time of night? Are you all right?"

"For the most part. Dr. Lund's been shot. She's dead. I didn't figure things out in time."

"Oh." She was silent a moment, quite a feat for my chatterbox. "I'm so sorry, Axe. Knowing you, you're blaming yourself for the murder. You aren't Sherlock Holmes. Close, maybe, but you've got a ways to go."

"I'm going over to Eben's for a while. Maybe all night."

"Poor Eben. She was his friend. I think he might have been sweet on her."

"I think they might have been more than just friends at one time."

"That makes it even sadder."

"It does, and he hired me to guard her. He was fool enough to trust me."

"Stop beating yourself up. Find out who killed Dr. Lund. That's the best you can do."

"I guess. Listen, I'll call you again later."

"Come for breakfast."

"Will the lovely Prissy May be there?"

"You're a monster. Go to Eben's. Take care of him. Take care of yourself. You're still my little onion fritter."

"You're still my greasy french-fry."

I drove over to Eben's. A lot of lights were on. He met me at the door before I could ring the bell.

"The snakes are all in bed. Come in. I've made coffee. Or, would you like something a little stronger?"

"Could you put a shot of whiskey in mine?"

"Of course. I was having a drink myself."

I followed him into the kitchen at the back of the house. In the little breakfast nook I drank whiskey-spiked coffee while Eben sipped sherry. There was a sheaf of photos on the table. All of Kirsten Lund, or Kirsten Lund and a much younger Eben. They'd been taken with a cheap snapshot camera. In every picture they were smiling.

"I just thought—I wanted to see her beautiful face again. I keep thinking—it's silly really—her leg will never heal now."

"No. I'm sorry. You were pretty close to her once, weren't you?"

He nodded. "More than close. In spite of the age difference, we fell in love, a long time ago. I would gladly have married her, but she wouldn't hear of it. She would never have married anyone. Later, when she and Ollie Crampton became a couple, I was a terribly jealous, bitter, man, Axe."

"That doesn't sound like you."

"It took me a long time to get over it. Eventually, Kirsten and I became good friends again, but of course things were not the same." He looked down at the photos on the table. "These pictures were taken when I was at my happiest. I like to think Kirsten was happy, too."

"I'll find who killed her, Eben," I said, feeling

suddenly angry. "I'll make sure whoever it is pays for Dr. Lund's murder. I just wish I could have prevented it."

"It wasn't your fault. You didn't murder Kirsten, some maniac did. I know you'll find them."

14

It was a long night for Eben and me. We stayed up until four or so. Then Eben led me to a guest room, with no snakes, and I crashed like an eighty-foot pine under the axe of a lumberjack. I slept until noon. When I got up and came downstairs, Eben was already fussing around in the kitchen with scrambled eggs, sausage, cheese Danish, and coffee. There was a copper-brown snake wrapped around his neck.

"It's only Geoffrey, a coach whip snake. He's quite polite and tame, and of course not poisonous. Do you mind if he joins us for breakfast?"

"Not if he's your buddy. But he better keep his scales off of my Danish."

"Deal. Let's eat."

We ate heartily. Nothing like death to make a man hungry. After breakfast, I left. Eben followed me to the door. I started to say something to him, but there was nothing to say. I patted him on the shoulder and he nodded, wiping away some mois-

ture from his eyes. I even said good-bye to Geoffrey.

Back home I made some coffee and nursed an
uncharacteristic hangover. I stretched out on the
bed and the phone rang. Never fails.

"Axe Hatchett."

"Hey, Axe Hatchett. It's your neighbor, Blythe.
Did you get in trouble last night?"

"Nothing I couldn't handle."

"I thought I'd let you know the Quartz Quarry
police are hot on the trail of Doc Lund's murder-
ers."

"There's more than one?"

"Maybe. We picked up those boys whose
names you gave us. Think you might have given
us those names a little sooner?"

"Honestly, I didn't know it was going to turn
out to be so important."

"They were at a party from eight until one in
the morning. Lots of witnesses, but they were
mostly drunk. The party was at a house only ten
blocks from Doc Lund's. Al or Ted could have
slipped away from the party long enough to shoot
the lady, then gone back. If anybody'd missed
them, they could have claimed they were outside
puking."

"You think they did it?"

"There doesn't appear to be much of a motive.
But one of them got scared and spilled his guts."

"Tell me about it."

"Seems Doc Lund hired those two to break into

her place and tear it apart. Then she asked them to dangle her out a window. They were supposed to drop her onto a pile of leaves, but I guess they got carried away. She overshot the leaves by a couple of yards. They got scared and ran away. They say that's the whole story, what they know of it. They said Lund told them she was going to make a false insurance claim, that she needed the money. What was wrong with that woman? Did she like pain? The wrong kind of excitement?"

"I didn't know her well enough to make a guess. I just wish I'd been able to stop it."

"You were doing your job and something bad happened. Not your fault. Happens to cops all the time. That's why they drink."

"Black Label?"

"Sometimes something stronger."

"If you find out anything interesting about the Lund murder, would you mind sharing it?"

"Up to a point, sure. We don't know much about it yet, though we do know she was shot with a thirty caliber bullet. Likely from a deer rifle. They found what was left of the slug in the wall opposite where Lund was rolling back and forth in her wheelchair. The slug's pretty beat up. Ballistics might not be able to do anything with it. It was a hollow-point, a hunting cartridge. It mushroomed pretty good. And since it had passed through Lund's skull before it hit the wall, it was pretty distorted."

"Might have come from a M1-Carbine, you

think?"

"I doubt it. The bullet was pointed. Those M1's don't cycle as well as you'd like. Folks generally load them up with round nosed-bullets."

"OK. Maybe something like a Winchester lever action carbine?"

"More than likely. God knows there are plenty of those around in this part of the country."

"I wonder, are either Ted or Al hunters?"

"We'll find out. We're nowhere near finished with those boys."

"Thanks for the information."

"Happy to oblige."

We ended our call. Now I needed to call Tracy. I knew I was in trouble with her. In dealing with the intricacies of the ivory ibis case I'd forgotten something very important. Tracy's wisdom tooth. She'd been scheduled to have it pulled yesterday, and dear old sensitive Axe had let it slip his mind entirely. If she wanted to, she could give me a pretty hard time of it. But she knew I was feeling bad about letting a murder take place right under my nose. Maybe she'd give me a break. I called her at Rocko's.

"Tracy," I said, when she answered the phone. "How's the wisdom tooth? Is it only a memory?"

"A bad memory, but not as bad as yours."

"It slipped my mind, and that's pretty inexcusable. Forgive me?"

"You've been busy, and not sleeping enough, and you're upset about Dr. Lund's death. Otherwise I wouldn't let you forget it for a long time."

"I'll make it up to you, my little burned waffle."

"Come over for breakfast."

"Thanks, but I ate at Eben's. Just the three of us. Me, Eben, and Geoffrey."

"Who's Geoffrey?"

"A cute-as-a-button coach whip snake."

"You must have loved that. Did he eat much?"

"No. He never got past his first cup of coffee."

"What's going on with the case?"

I told her what Blythe had passed on to me.

"You think those college kids killed Dr. Lund?"

"My gut says no. I'm going to have to talk to a couple of folks. Lilith, for one."

"She couldn't have done it."

"Of course not. But she might give me some information. Minnie might too. And I want to speak to Ollie Crampton."

"You're going to have a busy day. Stop by later."

"I will. Have you bought my Christmas present yet?"

"Yes. Have you bought mine?"

"Not yet, but I've picked it out."

"You better buy it before someone else does."

"Don't worry. The gift's being held in my name."

"Is it an airplane?"

"Yes, you guessed it! Listen, I better get back to work."

"A detective's job is never done."

"It's done when the case is solved. Maybe I'll see you at supper time."

"I'll save one of tomorrow's donuts for you."

"Swell."

We exchanged a sloppy kiss over the phone and rang off.

I decided to go visit the Lund house. I hoped the cops wouldn't still be there collecting pocket lint and gum wrappers to analyze. I chose not to call ahead. I liked taking people by surprise.

As I drove over to the scene of Kirsten Lund's murder, I thought about the fake robbery she'd staged. What was it about? I couldn't believe it was really only a case of insurance fraud, as Lund had apparently told her accomplices. Someone had hated her enough, or feared her enough, to kill her. Maybe the feeling had been mutual.

Was it possible that Dr. Lund had been trying to set up someone else's murder when she pretended to be attacked by treasure hunters? She could have broken into Ollie Crampton's house and killed Lilith—her rival—and made it look like the ivory ibis hunters had committed the crime. Or perhaps she was waiting for Crampton to come back from New Mexico so she could murder him. None of this made complete sense to me, but I had to come up with some kind of theory. I didn't want the trail leading to Lund's murderer to grow cold.

Minnie's Dodge and Lilith's Muntz were parked in their usual spots, but there were no cop cars in sight. I rang the bell and Minnie let me in. I was surprised to find Lilith in the living room. I'd figured she'd still be in the hospital. She looked a bit numb, maybe tired, but she greeted me with a slow smile.

"Welcome to our happy home," she said.

"You doing all right?"

"A little gun shy, and shocked. I still can't believe Kirsten's dead, and that I saw it happen."

"Sure. It's tough for you. What about you, Minnie? Are you holding up OK?"

"As well as can be expected."

I heard a chirping sound. I looked over to see what it was. There was a canary in a cage, on a small round table, directly in front of the living room window that had been shattered by the bullet that killed Lund. I noticed the window had already been re-glazed. Pretty fast service.

"I'm glad you got the window put back in," I said.

"Yes," said Minnie. "The college maintenance crew was kind enough to do that. I'm not even sure who called them."

"Where'd the canary come from?"

"I've had it for a couple of days. Lilith bought it for me. Wasn't that kind?"

"How's come I didn't notice it yesterday?"

"It was there. Its name is Tristan"

"That's interesting." I'd spent a year in a prison near San Francisco for a crime I didn't commit. The prison library had proved very interesting. In one of its books I'd read something about the story of Tristan and Isolde. "Weren't Tristan and Isolde an item, in mythology? I know of a stuffed burro named Isolde. And since burros in this part of the country are called Rocky Mountain canaries, that makes sense."

"Kirsten came up with the name. I was going to name him Pretty Boy."

"I've been a little absent-minded lately," I said, "but I'm sure that canary wasn't here yesterday."

"You put it in the bedroom yesterday, Minnie," said Lilith. "Don't you remember? Right before you went out to visit your sisters. I wish you hadn't; he'd been singing so beautifully."

"I didn't want Tristan to disturb you and Kirsten. I'm glad you mentioned my sisters." She turned to me. "I have two sisters in town. I made the rounds yesterday, and didn't get back until late. Not until — well, you know. They both gave me Christmas gifts. They're still in the car. I think I'll go get them right now."

She got out of her chair, fetched a winter coat from a hook near the front door, and went outside.

"Who killed her, Mr. Hatchett?" asked Lilith.

"Axe. I don't know yet. But I'm determined to find out. Is Ollie home today, do you suppose?"

"You surely don't think Ollie killed Kirsten. He loved her."

"He's not a suspect. I just want to ask him a few questions."

Minnie returned, carrying an armload of brightly-wrapped packages. She put them down under the small Christmas tree that occupied one corner of the living room. Then she stood there, shivering in her coat.

"It's getting colder out. I hope it won't snow any more. It makes driving so hard," she said. She stuck her hands into her coat pockets, frowned. Then she pulled something small out of one pocket. There was a flash of bright metal. Probably a lipstick. She let it drop back into her pocket and took off her coat and hung it back on its hook.

Lilith stood up. "I've got to get out of here. I'm sorry, Minnie, I can't stay here right now. I'll be back in time for dinner. My turn to cook, right?"

"Are you going over to Professor Crampton's?"

"No. I'm going to the college. I've got some things to do in my office, before next semester starts. Might as well get started now. Good bye, Mr. Hatchett."

"Actually, I should be going myself. I just stopped by to check on things. Minnie, I'll see you later."

Lilith and I left together.

"That's quite a car you've got," I told her, gesturing at the blue Muntz.

"Thank you. It was a gift from my folks. I really wish they wouldn't buy me such expensive gifts, but they don't seem able to stop themselves. I see you don't have well-off relatives like I have." She pointed at Tracy's old Chevy.

"That's the kind of car I like to drive. It runs

great, but it's as inconspicuous as a car could be."

We bid each other good-bye and got in our cars, Lilith to presumably go to her office at Flinders College, and me to pay an unexpected visit to Ollie Crampton.

15

There were a couple of things about him that bothered me. On the night of the shooting, last night, he had been awfully interested in where I was going to park my car while I watched Lund's house. Why? Maybe because he wanted to make sure I wouldn't be able to see him when he shot Kirsten.

Whoever had shot her had made sure I couldn't see what was happening. Ollie also seemed the type of guy who might own a thirty-thirty carbine. It sounded like he spent a good deal of his time out in the wilderness, by himself, on his archeological digs. Aside from occasional screwy people, he'd also have to watch out for mountain lions, possibly hungry bears.

But why would he want to kill Kirsten, his colleague and old lover? Because she was trouble to him. She was jealous of his romantic involvement with Lilith. If Kirsten had been planning to murder Lilith, and I suspected that was the case, then she might have had plans to harm Ollie as well. Maybe not murder. Maybe something else. Like destroying his career by exposing a scandal.

Crampton's silver-and-red Willys was parked out in front of his house. When I rang the bell, it took a good two minutes before he answered. I was getting ready to push the bell again when the door jerked open.

"I was taking a shower," he complained, before he even saw who I was.

"Either you take a lot of showers, or I need to work on my timing," I told him.

To my surprise, he laughed, a good long roar that showed lots of back teeth.

"Come in, shamus, come in."

The place looked the same as the last time I'd seen it. Neat and orderly in a confused, over-stuffed, kind of way. We sat down in the living room and he offered me coffee.

"Sure. Black. Thanks."

He disappeared into the kitchen and came back with two steaming mugs.

"Are you here to tell me something about Kirsten's murder? Or are you here to ask questions?"

"I wish I had some information to offer you, but I don't. I'm just poking around, hoping I'll stumble across some information worth having."

"I don't know if I can help you then." He shook his big, handsome head. Behind his spectacles his eyes misted over. "You probably run across murdered people all the time," he said, "if you're any-thing like movie detectives. But has a good friend of yours ever been murdered?"

"As a matter of fact, yes."

"Then I guess you know how I feel. I'm not on-ly saddened, and shocked, I'm damned angry."

"I understand. And believe me—and I know this firsthand too—you'll feel a lot better when the person who killed her is behind bars, or sitting in the hot seat."

"I guess that's where you come in, right?"

"Sure, but I could use some help."

"I'll tell you anything I know."

"Swell. Let's start with this: can you think of anybody who would have wanted Dr. Lund dead?"

"Kirs? Well, she could rub people the wrong way sometimes. But, murder? No."

"I hate to point this out, but you could end up being a suspect. I'm talking about the cops, not me."

"That's crazy. Why would I kill Kirs?"

"Start with the Green-Eyed Monster."

He threw himself back in his chair, noisily drank some coffee. Then he took a pipe and tobac-co from a table at his elbow and made a big show of packing the pipe and lighting it. He finally quit stalling and started talking.

"Here's the whole story," he said. "Kirs and I were a couple for years. She was something spe-cial. I even considered marrying her, which is pretty amazing for me. But, you know what? She refused me. Said she wasn't the marrying kind. And then, well, Lilith joined the English department.

"All the red-blooded profs went goofy over her. You've seen her. But it isn't just her looks. She's a fascinating person. A damned good teacher and researcher, too. She did all the right things. She went from assistant, to associate, to full professor in record time.

"Kirs hated her for it. You see, Dr. Lund had some issues. She could never get past being an associate. She had only herself to blame, though I'm sorry to say it. She got in fights with the department head, made passes at her own students, developed strange illnesses—fake ones—that let her take time off. You name it, she was a mess. But she was also a great teacher. Ask any of her students. So the college hung onto her.

"After we'd been together for a few years we had a big fight. I never even quite understood what it was about. She broke up with me. And Lilith was waiting in the wings. Beautiful, charming, reasonable, bright as a new penny. Kirs could never forgive the two of us. In fact, she tried pretty hard to get me in trouble, and came damned close to succeeding."

"Tell me about that, if you don't mind."

"I'm an archaeologist, and an anthropologist. I love going out on digs. And I often go by myself. About a year ago, I was out at a dig in southern

Colorado. I came across some pretty interesting stuff, and I spent a lot of time hiking through the deserts and canyons looking for artifacts. I found an old cliff dwelling, a small one, and it looked like no one had ever picked it over. I brought back some potshards, some fragments of baskets, and some other artifacts.

"When I got home, I started going over my maps to see just exactly where I'd been. Turns out, I'd trespassed on Indian lands. It was an accident. I'm not a thief. I returned everything I'd taken and even talked to the Ute Indian Council about what I'd inadvertently done. They weren't happy, but they left me alone.

"Well, I'd made the mistake of telling Kirsten the whole story. Before I knew what was going on, she'd managed to poison the whole department against me. She could have ruined my career at the college. She could have destroyed my credibility as an archeologist. Who would have paid any attention to me? Who would have read my papers?"

"That must have made you pretty mad."

"I'll say. Kirs and I were never close after that, though I couldn't help but remain her friend, what with our history."

"Did Lund try to hurt Umbray in any way?"

"Lilith is squeaky clean, but I'm sure Kirsten would have blackened her name if she'd gotten the chance."

"When Dr. Lund broke her leg you came running to help her. Can you explain that?"

He shrugged. "Maybe I thought it might mean something to Kirs." He threw back his head and laughed again. "Besides, I loved the idea of Kirsten showing up at a department Christmas party just a day after being attacked and having her leg broken."

"What do you think about that whole ivory ibis business? Do you think that attack on Dr. Lund was on the square?"

"What do you mean?"

"Listen, I've got some information, but the cops have it too. I don't think they'd want me sharing it with you or anyone else."

"Come on, Hatchett! I just spilled my guts for you. You've got no right holding back information from me."

"It's not the same, Ollie. I'm gathering information to try to find out who killed Dr. Lund. If I'm helping the cops keep a couple of secrets, I'm doing it for the same reason. Let me just say there were one or two things wrong with the crime scene after Lund was attacked."

He thought about it, fingering the lapel of the bath robe he was wearing. "Do you mean the attack was faked?"

"Maybe. But I'm not telling you anything else. Instead, I'm going to ask you a question you aren't going to like, so don't get up on your hind legs. Do you own a rifle?"

"I see. Kirs was shot with a rifle. Yes, I own

two."

"What kind and caliber?"

"I've got an old twenty-two that belonged to my dad. And I've also got a Winchester thirty-thirty."

"Where are they?"

"The twenty-two's in the hall closet. I left the thirty-thirty at the ranch house I used as my bivouac down at my dig in New Mexico."

"OK. Listen, I don't think I have any more questions. I'll let you get back to your shower." I stood up to go. Crampton stood up as well. "Wait," I said, "one more question. Why did you want to know where I was going to park last night, when I was watching Dr. Lund's house?"

Ollie shrugged. "I guess I was kind of telling you how to do your job. Sorry. I just wanted to make sure you were in a position to see any prowlers who might come around the house. Obviously you couldn't keep an eye on the entire house. I agreed with you about parking where you could see both the front and side windows of the living room, as well as the outside door."

"OK. That makes sense."

"Have you talked to Lilith yet?" he asked.

"A little. I just came from Minnie's."

"I don't like the fact that I'm a suspect, though I guess I can understand it. I guess you already know this. You were there for part of it. Lilith told me about the gun play between her and Kirsten at Minnie's the other day. I just want you to know

Kirs started the whole thing. She pulled a gun on her. Lilith was just defending herself."

"I'll keep it in mind, Doc. But if you're thinking Lilith might be considered a suspect, forget it. Her alibi couldn't be better. Though I guess she could have hired someone to kill Dr. Lund. Thanks for your time, and for being so cooperative."

"I have no reason to not cooperate."

"If you think of anything that might help solve this case, let me know."

"I will. I won't shower again until I hear from you."

"Listen, could I borrow your phone a minute?"

"Help yourself. It's on the table there. I'll give you some privacy." He stepped into his kitchen. I called Rocko's. The dulcet chimes that Prissy May used for a voice answered. I asked for my little stuffed mushroom cap.

"Axe?" Tracy screeched.

"Yes. Listen, Christmas Eve is tomorrow. I'm still in the middle of this damned case."

"You aren't getting out of having Christmas at my folks."

"Of course not. But I've got a problem. I know we'd planned to open our presents to each other at your folks' house, but my present to you is a bit — inconvenient. Could I give it to you today?"

"What'd you get me?"

"You'll see. Can I bring it over to Rocko's in a little bit?"

"Sure. Do you want me to have yours ready?"

"That'd be swell. Give it a good wax job before I get there."

"It's not a car, though it cost an arm and a leg."

"Yours or Prissy May's?"

"We're getting along fine now. I might have found another job. Mom just called me."

"Great. I hope you get it. It's nothing like Rocko's, is it?"

"No, it's a mom and pop sandwich shop, though they serve breakfast too. And, you know what?"

"What?"

"The sandwich shop's located in a two-story building. The downstairs has some office space next to the restaurant, and the upstairs is an apartment. They're both for rent. What do you think? You could have your office downstairs and we could live in the apartment."

"I think I want to see this place. How's the rent?"

"I don't know. We'll have to ask."

"Let's hope it's good and cheap. I've got to go. I'll be over in a little while."

We made kissy noises over the phone, like a couple of goofs, and hung up. I used the phone again to call Blythe Bliss at the police station.

"Bliss."

"This is Axe. Say, you aren't by any chance one of those people who hide house keys under door-mats, or in flower pots, or something?"

"Might could be. Why?"

"I'd like to pick up my kittens and take them over to Tracy."

"You got cat litter and food?"

"I'll buy some right away."

"OK. I'm going to whisper to you where I keep a spare key. It's under a rock halfway between the house and the elm tree."

"How many paces from the house? Can I find it without a full moon?"

"It's easy to find. Just follow the instructions."

"You sure you don't mind my creeping around your place when you aren't there?"

"Don't take anything, especially not the beer."

"I'll resist the urge. Thanks."

"Bye now."

There was a pet shop between my house and Ollie's. I drove over there. When I stepped inside the shop, I was hit by the smell of stale monkey and gone-bad goldfish. Right near the front window was a glass terrarium with a big black-and-white snake in it. A label on the glass said it was a King snake and not to tap on the glass. They wanted eight dollars for it. Were they crazy?

I bought a bag of cat litter, a tray to put it in, and some kitten chow. Then I drove home and began the search for Blythe's key. I turned over three rocks before I found it. Inside the cottage, I rounded up my cat couple, let them say good-bye to mama, and went to my place. I'd been saving a good-sized cardboard box with a lid for just this occasion. I poked some holes in the lid and put my captives inside.

The kittens stayed pretty quiet on our way over to Rocko's death pit. I parked directly in front and carried the box inside. Prissy May turned on her best smile. At least, I hope it was her best. Her male customers would have a hard time standing up to anything brighter or sweeter.

"Merry Christmas!" I said to Tracy.

"And a merry Christmas to you, my little collapsed plum pudding."

I set the box on the counter. I'd left the litter and food in the car. Tracy handed me a brightly but clumsily-wrapped present about the size of my hand. It was heavy.

"You first," I said.

"Is it a pet rat?"

"Close. Lift the lid."

She pulled off the lid, took one look at the kittens, and started bawling.

"I can take them back," I said, hastily. "Maybe you'd rather have a mink coat."

She shook her head and tenderly lifted one of the kittens from the box. The mean-looking one.

"When I was a little girl," she said, "I caught an alley cat, just a half grown kitten. I named it Chrysanthemum."

"You didn't?"

She nodded.

"One day she ran away and I never saw her again." More tears. "I've always wanted another cat, but I never dared get one."

"We won't let these guys run away. We'll put leg irons on them if we have to. And please don't name either of them Chrysanthemum."

"That would be bad luck."

"Yeah. Besides, they're both boys. What do you think you might name them?"

"I don't know. I'll have to be around them for a while before I can decide on names. Thank you, Axe."

"Sure. I got cat litter and food and stuff in the car. I'll get it in a minute. You going to keep these kids upstairs until we get our own place?"

"I'll keep them behind the counter when I'm working."

"Don't let Cookie mistake them for a couple of pounds of hamburger."

"I won't let him near them." She took the second kitten, the ugliest one, from the box. The two of them walked around on the counter, perfectly happy. Prissy May made squealing and cooing sounds.

"They're so adorable," she said.

"You be careful with them," Tracy warned her. "They're fragile."

"I'm glad you like them," I said to Tracy.

"I love them. Now, open your gift."

I tore the paper off my present and stared at it. How the hell did Tracy come up with the money for it? It was a beautiful nickel-plated revolver, a Smith and Wesson Centennial. I'd never even seen one before except in a gun shop. It had a black rubber grip and a holster I could wear inside my pants waistband. It had a shrouded hammer so that it could only be fired by pulling the trigger double action. But the most interesting feature about it was the grip safety. It was made like the old Smith and Wesson lemon squeezer. There was a spring-loaded dingus on the back of the grip. To shoot the gun you had to get a good grip on it first.

"Tracy, it's a swell gun, it really is. But I can't keep it."

"Then take your kittens back." More tears.

"You can't afford a gun like this."

"I didn't steal it. Mom loaned me the money. I'll pay her back. I wanted you to have a really safe revolver. I don't want you shooting yourself. I'm not taking it back. You're stuck with it."

"It's terrific. Thanks. Every time I shoot it I'll think of you."

"That's so romantic. Load it."

"What? Now?"

"Yes. I want you to start carrying it right away. You can put your old one in the glove box of the Nash."

I pulled my Chief's Special, swung out the cylinder and dumped the cartridges into my palm. Then I set the Chief's on the counter and loaded the shells into my new Centennial. While I was doing this, a customer, a grayish, drab-faced, guy, came through the door. He saw Prissy May's smile, then he saw the guns on the counter, and he backed out of the place without having even taken off his hat.

"Oh, I hope he comes back," said Prissy May.

"I guess he didn't like all the hardware," I said. I put my new revolver in its holster and clipped it inside my pants. It felt good. Tracy beamed.

"I got to get back to work," I said. "Let me go get the cat litter and stuff. Oh, and thanks a million for the new gat. You shouldn't have, but it's a nifty piece."

When I returned from the car, Tracy was looking around for something soft to put in the cardboard box for the nameless kittens to sleep on.

"What about that nice new sweater you wore to work?" she asked Prissy May.

"Oh, yes, my sweater." Prissy May's smile faded for half a second. "Sure, Tracy, my sweater will work great."

"I've got to be going," I said. Tracy gave me a kiss on the mouth that was hardly chaste and I left.

16

Even though I was in the car, driving, I wasn't sure where I was going. An elusive thought was loitering in my head, but I couldn't get a handle on it. For some reason I started thinking about that damned King snake I'd seen in Paradise Pets. I'd told Eben that if the name of the old gold miner's burro, Isolde, turned out to be the key to solving the ivory ibis case, I'd buy him a new snake. I slammed on my brakes, even though I was right in the middle of traffic. Fortunately, no one ran into me, though I got a nice Christmas honk from the guy directly in back of me.

Minnie's canary was named Tristan. She kept him on a table near the living room window — for the sun, I suppose. But she'd moved the feathered warbler before going out on the day Lund was shot. Why? Perhaps so the bird cage wouldn't be in the way when Minnie fired a high-powered rifle through the window to kill her landlady. She'd gone out to visit two sisters, in different parts of town. She could have visited the first sister, driven over and killed Lund, and gone on to the second sister's. It would have taken only a few minutes to commit the murder. She had an alibi that would work just fine.

Opportunity was there, but what about motive? Well, she liked Lilith, and, like all the ladies, she had a yen for Ollie. She knew that Kirsten had threatened Lilith with a gun only the day before. And she may have suspected that there was something funny about the whole treasure hunters' attack. But did she own a rifle, and could she shoot?

She'd claimed to be afraid of guns, but that could have been a cover if she was already thinking of protecting Ollie and Lilith. Lots of folks have guns tucked away in closets or under their beds. Especially in the Wild West where I live. Still, I wanted to find out for sure before I accused Minnie of murder. It'd be rude otherwise. I stopped at a pay phone and called Crampton. He answered on the second ring.

"I hope you weren't taking another shower," I said, when he picked up.

"Not while you're still in town. I plan on staying dirty."

"I've got an odd question for you, and don't read too much into it. OK?"

"All right. What's the question."

"How well do you know Minnie?"

"Not too well, I guess. She's the English Department's secretary. Not my department. But she's been around awhile and so have I. Why?"

"Would you happen to know if she's a hunter?"

"Minnie? No, I don't think so. She grew up on a ranch near here, so I'm sure her dad hunted. Wait, you don't think she shot Kirs, do you?"

"I asked you not to read too much into the question. Would you happen to have Lilith's office number at the college?"

"Lilith isn't responsible for Kirs's death. I'm certain of it."

"I agree with you, but she might know more about Minnie than you do."

"I've got her office number in my little black book. Let me fetch it."

He was off the line for a minute.

"Here it is." He gave me the number. I said good-bye and dialed Umbray's number.

"Hello?"

"Lilith? This is Axe Hatchett. I've got a question for you, and don't read too much into it."

"I'll try not to."

"Would you happen to know if Minnie owns a rifle?"

The line was silent for several seconds. "It's strange you should ask that. When I was moving into Kirsten's place, Minnie told me I could hang my winter coat and things in the hall closet in her own apartment. I had to make room; she has a lot of coats and things in there. I noticed an old gun leaning against the wall. I don't know if it was a rifle or a shotgun. I was a little surprised. Minnie had once told me she was afraid of guns because once, when she was still living on her family's ranch, she mistook her brother for a deer and almost shot him. But you don't think — ?"

"Never mind what I think. With you and Lund hanging around in the living room, when could Minnie have found a time to take that rifle out of the closet and put it someplace else?"

"Well, I was in and out of the house. And Kirsten had to go to the bathroom sometime. Though I don't know how she managed to hoist herself out of the wheelchair and onto the toilet seat with that cast."

"Swell. Thanks for the information. Listen, don't do something silly like calling the cops, or anyone else. I want to handle this myself. It requires delicacy."

"You don't strike me as delicate, but I'll keep my mouth shut. My God, I knew Minnie hated Kirsten, but would she actually kill her?"

"Maybe to protect you and Ollie. She hated Lund?"

"Maybe hate's too strong a word. Kirsten was kind of full of herself as a professor. She gave Minnie a pretty hard time as secretary. In fact, she tried to get her fired more than once. Kirsten thought Minnie was incompetent and a gossip."

"That could make a person hate you. Listen, I got to go."

"Don't you dare not call me if you find something out. I gather you want me to stay away from

Minnie's place for a while."

"That would be a good idea. Merry Christmas! Good bye."

So Minnie had opportunity, motive, and maybe a rifle. I drove over to her place again. On the way, I thought about how she might have managed things.

Minnie's bedroom was at the back of the house. On the night of the murder she could have grabbed the rifle from under the bed or wherever, lowered it out of her window, and leaned it against the outside house wall. Then, when she left the girls for the evening, she could have driven her Dodge up the alley and retrieved the gun. It was still daylight, so she would have had to be careful, but there were plenty of trees in the back-yard to thwart the view of nosey neighbors.

She could have driven over to sister number one's house, had a nice long visit, and then driven back to Lund's. She knew where I was parked. Driving back through the alley, she could have crept around the side of the house, shot Lund through the window, and walked back to her car, carrying the rifle under her coat, barrel down, stock tucked under her arm pit, if it was indeed a short gun, a carbine.

Then she could have visited sister number two. Merry Christmas, Sis, sorry I'm a little late. That was pretty nervy, but some people are just made to be killers. Where had she hidden the gun afterwards? I would have loved to know that.

I reached Lund's and parked the car. I made sure my new Centennial was within easy reach: I pulled it from its holster and transferred it to my overcoat pocket. Minnie must have been staring out her window. Once again she opened the door before I could ring the bell. She was wearing an apron with pockets. Don't tell me the woman was doing housework?

"Mr. Hatchett. Back so soon?"

"Couldn't stay away."

She invited me in. We both sat down.

"I've got a friend on the police force," I said.

"That must be convenient for you, in your line of work."

"Sure. Sometimes I pick up a little information before the general public reads about it in the papers. You're sunk, Minnie. You have a nosey neighbor."

"Do I? Which one?"

"The one who finally confessed to the cops that she saw you shoot Dr. Lund through the window. Ring a bell?"

She stood up.

"That's ridiculous. No one saw me—I didn't shoot Dr. Lund. How dare you! There's some mistake."

"Yeah, but you're the one who made it. You didn't make your escape quick enough. You had to go and look for the cartridge case you jacked out of your rifle. It took you a few seconds. And during that time your neighbor looked out the window, wondering what that big noise had been. Was it a car backfiring? No. It was you killing a woman you hated, trying to protect your friends, Lilith and Ollie."

"I want you to leave. If the police have anything to say to me, they'll contact me."

"They don't have to. They're on their way, and I'm not budging."

To my amazement, she pulled a gun from her apron pocket. It was that same damned Iver Johnson I'd loaned to Lund. I wondered why the cops didn't have it. Maybe Minnie had taken the guns away from the ladies after their showdown and stashed them someplace. She pointed the revolver at my gizzard.

"Kirsten deserved to die, and I'm sure she was going to kill Ollie and Lilith. She was crazy. Now, what am I going to do about you?"

"Shoot me, I guess."

I saw her finger tighten on the trigger.

17

I pulled the Centennial out of my pocket. There was no time to aim. I shot from the hip. Both guns exploded at once. I felt something hit my ribs just as I saw Minnie drop the gun and grab at a red spot on her left shoulder. I stepped forward and knocked her down and grabbed the gun from the floor.

She didn't look badly hurt, but she was crying and cursing. My ribs felt on fire. I did a little cursing myself. Then I found the phone and called the cops. They said they'd send a squad car and call the hospital to send an ambulance.

I went to the kitchen and found a couple of hand towels, then went back to the living room and gave one of the towels to Minnie. She pressed it to her wound. I unbuttoned my overcoat and pressed my towel to my wound. We were quite the pair. Minnie had pulled herself up to a sitting position on the floor, her back to the couch.

"You're a good detective," she snarled at me.

"I'll give you that."

"I appreciate the compliment." I grabbed the phone and called Rocko's. Tracy answered.

"I just tried out my new gun, sugar lump. It works great."

"Were you shooting tin cans?"

"No, a murderess. I just winged her. But she got me back. Nothing serious. A broken rib, maybe. The cops will be here pretty soon, then I guess me and Annie Oakley will be going to the hospital."

"What? The hospital? I'll meet you there." She hung up.

A siren wailed up the street and in a few moments a black-and-white pulled to the curb out front. The cops were barely in the house before the ambulance pulled up. A couple of the officers questioned me and Minnie while the ambulance crew fussed over us, then we all went off to the hospital together. Tracy was waiting in the emergency room for me. She glared at Minnie as they wheeled her by on a gurney. Then she glared at the cops when they told her she couldn't talk to me.

"He's my fiancé, and he's hurt. I'll talk to him all I want. Why don't you go arrest some jay walkers or something?"

"He's part of a shooting investigation, ma'am," said a tubby officer with caterpillar eyebrows. "We got to question him. We don't need no witnesses."

"No? What about the doctors and the nurses?"

"That's different. They work here and they need to do their jobs."

"What if I told you I was a nurse? Look at my smock, I've got blood all over it."

"That's ketchup, lady. Stand aside."

"Come on, leave her be," I said. "She's my partner. She's my operative."

The big bluff guy in blue who'd been trying to stand in Tracy's way took a good look at her face and backed down.

"OK. OK. But you can't talk."

The cops and Tracy clustered around while a nurse and a doctor young enough to be a Boy Scout worked me over. They peeled my shirt and undershirt off, picked some pieces of cloth out of the wound with tweezers, scoured it out with alcohol, and argued about whether or not they should extract the slug.

They decided they better, so they stuck some kind of medical needle-nosed pliers in the hole and dug around until they'd managed to excavate the flattened slug. I was lucky. I'd only been shot with a thirty-two. It had passed through my overcoat and both my shirts and lodged its sweet self between a couple of my ribs. It was painful, but not serious.

I heard later that Minnie wasn't so lucky. My thirty-eight bullet had broken off the end of her collar bone and exited through the back of her shoulder blade. It'd take a while to heal, but she'd type again someday. Maybe the prison could find a secretarial spot for her. Maybe she could work for the warden. Better that than the laundry.

"Why do you always have to get yourself shot?" Tracy complained.

"What do you mean? I've only been shot twice since I met you."

"I should have bought you a bullet-proof vest."

"There's always my birthday."

A nurse with the disposition of a bull moose gave me a shot and I was moved to a hospital room. I didn't plan on being there Christmas day. I'd pull a Lund and disappear. I asked a nurse if I could get a phone in my room and she said no, but she helped me down the hall to the nurses' station and I used the phone there. I called Lilith and told her what was going on. Then I called Eben.

"I owe you a snake," I told him.

"Splendid. You solved the case, and Isolde was the magic word?"

"Correct."

"So I'll be getting that green mamba?"

"Not with my dime. If you want a serpent that packs its own poison, you'll have to buy it yourself."

"Who murdered Kirsten?"

"Minnie."

"Minnie? I didn't know she had it in her. Such a quiet, peaceable, secretary. Why did she do it?"

"Bunch of reasons. She believed Lund was going to try to kill Lilith and Crampton, or at least ruin them somehow. And she apparently didn't cotton to Lund. Be careful how you treat your secretaries."

"I'm shocked. Surely she was wrong. Kirsten wouldn't have killed anyone."

"She set up that whole fake attack on herself, I know that. There had to be a reason. If she hadn't broken her leg she might have killed Lilith and made it look like the treasure hunters did it. I'm sorry, Eben, but maybe you didn't know her as well as you thought."

"I was always fairly dazzled by her beauty. Among other things."

"I figured."

"But you solved the case. I owe you a debt of thanks. I don't feel any better, yet, but perhaps I will eventually. I also owe you money. Get my bill ready."

"Nothing doing. This one's on me. I failed you. I didn't protect your friend."

"I will pay you for solving the case. That's my final word."

"We'll see. I'm calling from the hospital. Minnie and I exchanged bullets for Christmas. We're both going to be OK. I'll drop by to see you as soon as I can get out of this torture chamber."

"Don't leave until you're well. I'm so sorry you've been injured. But at least you're going to be all right. I could have lost two friends."

"I'm glad you didn't." We ended the conversation.

The hospital was kind enough to let me loose

on Christmas Eve morning. Tracy picked me up in the Nash since her Chevy was still over at the Lund house. I tried to get Tracy to drop me off so I could get the car back, but she refused.

"You aren't doing any driving yet. You're hurt. You need to rest those ribs, poor critter."

"Then you'll have to help me run an errand."

"Gladly. Where to? The meter's running."

"Let's see if Paradise Pets is open on Christmas Eve." I told her how to get to the place.

"Is that where you got our kittens?"

"No. I bought them from a cop. Which reminds me, I owe her money. The cost of the kittens goes to the police relief fund. Mind if I give them ten bucks?"

"Sure. Cops need relief."

We arrived at the pet shop. They were open, though only until noon according to a sign on the door. We went inside. There was a young fellow feeding fish near the front of the shop.

"I want that damned King snake," I told him.

"A gift?"

"How'd you know?"

"I'll be happy to sell you that snake, but there's something you should know about it."

"Yeah? Does it walk with a limp?"

"No, but it gives off a God-awful stink if you scare it."

"I won't tell it any ghost stories. It's for a friend, a snake fancier. He'll know what to do to keep the slithery thing from blasting him with its stench.

How about seven bucks instead of eight?"

The kid shook his head. "I'd have to ask the owner, and he's not here. I'll have to charge the full eight. But I could throw a feeder mouse in for free."

"Nothing doing. I'm not going to be responsible for some poor mouse getting eaten by a snake. It's Christmas Eve, for God's sake. But can you give me a cardboard box to put the thing in?"

"I can, and I'll put some wood shavings in the bottom."

"Thanks."

He fetched the box from a backroom, then picked the snake up with some kind of tongs and dumped it in the box. He put the lid on.

"It won't need holes punched in it if you aren't going far."

"Just across town. What scares this thing, anyhow?"

"I don't know. I'd just be careful if I were you."

"I'll carry him on my lap," said Tracy.

"Better yours than mine." I paid for the snake and we went out to the car.

Tracy was as good as her word. All the way over to Eben's, she held the box on her lap while I drove. So much for me not driving. She kept making cooing sounds at the snake.

"Maybe I should have bought you a cobra instead of kittens," I complained.

"No, I love our kittens."

"Any ideas about names yet?"

"I'm still thinking."

"What about that job your mom told you about? Did you find out anything more about it?"

"I called the folks who own the sandwich shop. They own the whole building. They want to talk to me."

"Why don't we go over today? I want to see the place, and I want you to talk to the owners."

"How about after we leave Eben's?"

"Good idea."

We reached Eben's house and rang his doorbell. When he opened the door I noticed he was looking a couple of years older than he'd looked only a few days ago. But his eyes weren't red, and he greeted us with some show of cheerfulness.

"You've brought your lovely fiancée, Axe. Charming as ever. How are you Tracy? Welcome to my simple home."

"I'm fine. Are the snakes loose?" she asked, eagerly.

"They're napping."

"Good," I said. "We've brought them a new playmate, and I want to leave the introductions to you."

Tracy handed him the box. He sniffed at it.

"I think I recognize the breed," he said. "The King snake has a distinctive aroma." He lifted the lid of the box. "Ah, I was right. What a festive looking fellow he is, and quite a good size."

"How do you know it's a fellow?" I asked, because I really wanted to know.

"I won't know until I've done a cloaca probe."

"Sounds damned personal."

"Oh, it is. I'm just guessing this is a male because of its size. Care for coffee?"

"We've got to run," I said. "I just wanted to drop off the snake I owed you. How're things going for you?"

His face saddened.

"I'm still shocked and heart-broken by Kirsten's passing. But I'll get over it. What you told me about her wanting to possibly murder Lilith and Ollie is horrifying. I must give it some thought. Thank you, Axe, for honoring our bet and presenting me with this adorable King snake. And thank you for coming along, Tracy. You're like a ray of sunlight."

"That stuff's going to go to her head if you keep it up," I warned.

"You keep your mouth shut," Tracy told me.

We said our goodbyes and left.

18

"Do you know the address of the folks you're supposed to talk to about the job?"

"I've got it in my purse." Tracy carries a handbag the size of something a ten-year-old girl might carry. She dug in it and pulled out a crumpled piece of paper. "Keep driving, I'll tell you how to get there."

Twenty minutes later we were back on Rocko's side of town. Tracy had me pull up in front of a square brick building painted white. Big white letters in the front window proclaimed the place to be "Ben and Allie's Made to Order Sandwiches and Breakfasts." The other half of the downstairs had windows that were soaped over. We went inside.

It smelled good. Several customers sat on stools at a counter. There were also a handful of little tables. A second glassed-in counter displayed sandwiches wrapped in waxed paper, each one labeled. A slightly elderly couple stood behind the counters and beamed at us as we walked in. They were both short and plump and wore aprons and little white caps.

"Can we help you?" the man asked. "A sandwich maybe?"

He had some kind of accent but I couldn't tell what kind.

"We have sandwiches made just this morning, or we can make you a fresh one," said the woman. She had the same kind of accent.

"I'm here to talk about the waitressing job you advertised," said Tracy.

"I'm here to watch her," I said.

Both husband and wife clapped their hands simultaneously.

"So happy," said the man. "We need help. You see how busy we are. I am Ben and this, my wife, is Allie."

"Pleased to meet you. I'm Tracy Clover, and this is my fiancé, Axel."

"Oh, the so happy couple," cried Ally. They both clapped hands again.

"Let us talk about the job," said Ben. "But you are hungry, are you not? A sandwich? Chips? Pickles? Cookies? Coffee or lemonade?"

"Do you have egg salad?" I asked.

"Yes. Already made up."

"Do you have corned beef on rye?" asked Tracy.

"We'll make one in a jiffy. Chips?"

"Chips for me," I said.

"I'll take pickles."

"Good. Find a table you like. We'll bring you the food."

We found a table in a back corner and sat down. The chairs were comfortable. In no more than two minutes Ben brought us our food.

"I'd like some coffee, too, if you don't mind," I said.

"Yes, of course. And for you, Miss?"

"A lemonade, please."

"In a jiffy."

I bit into my sandwich. The bread tasted fresh baked, and the egg salad was great. Tracy tried her sandwich.

"Beats hell out of anything Rocko's has to offer," she said.

Ben returned with our drinks. "We are so busy, I'm sorry. You eat quiet for a while. OK? I'll talk to you when I can."

"We're in no hurry," I said.

We were finishing up our lunches before Ben returned to our table.

"So sorry. We're so busy. I have a favor to ask of you, Tracy. If you wouldn't mind. Could you help Allie while I talk to your fellow? Just pretend you're a waitress here already."

"Sure," said Tracy. "You got an apron I can borrow?"

"On the wall behind the counter."

Tracy jumped up and ran behind the counter. She tied on an apron and gave me a goofy smile.

"A good girl, no?"

"The best. You couldn't go wrong hiring Tracy. That reminds me. As soon as we get married, we're going to need a place, an apartment. And I'm looking for a new office. The place I've got now is all right, but it's not a great location."

"Such a coincidence. Allie and me own the whole building. Next door is what was a lawyer's office. He's retired now. Upstairs is a nice apartment. Not big, but nice. They're both for rent."

"While my girl's helping out your wife, could we take a look at the office and apartment?"

"Sure we could. I get the keys. I tell Allie."

He went back behind the counter, spoke to his wife, and grabbed some keys from the cash register drawer. I looked at Tracy. She was still smiling, and speaking sweetly to a customer. I wondered if Prissy May had rubbed off on her. Ben returned to me.

"This way. I show you."

We went out the front door and into the door of the office space. It was dim with the big window soaped over. Ben turned on a ceiling light. It was a good-sized room, but bare. No rug on the floor, no pictures on the walls, no furniture.

"A good big office," said Ben. "You could use it for a waiting room. What is it you do?"

"I'm a private investigator."

"Oh! Exciting. Let me show you the back room."

We walked through a doorway and into a room

slightly smaller and darker than the first.

"You could keep your desk here. Bookcases. A gun rack. Yes?"

"You bet. The place looks like it might do. Now I'd like to see the apartment."

"This way."

We went back outside and through a door located between the shop and the office. We climbed a flight of steep stairs and passed through another door. We were in a big living room, dining room, combination. In back of this room was a small kitchen, and next to it a bathroom. All clean and in good repair. We went back into the living room and through a door in the inside wall. It was a small bedroom with a window at the back. We went back into the living room and passed through a second door in the same wall. A bigger bedroom with a window in front. The place was pretty nice.

"You like?" asked Ben.

"It's swell. I want Tracy to see it."

"Yes, sure."

"What kind of rent are you asking?"

"For the office and the apartment, together, one-hundred-fifty a month. Good, yes?"

"Sounds about right. We could move in right away?"

His face clouded briefly. "Not until after you're married."

"Of course. We're getting hitched New Year's Day."

"Actually?"

"Yes."

"What a nice way to start your new year."

We went back downstairs and into the sandwich shop. The customers were beginning to thin out now. Tracy still had a smile plastered on her face. Allie was smiling too. We went over to them.

"Hire her, Ben. Tracy is good, like a daughter."

"For you, Allie, of course I will hire her." He turned to Tracy. "You want the job?"

"Boy, do I. This place is great. I can't wait to get away from Rocko's."

"Have you worked there long?"

"Three years."

"But you are not happy?"

"Cookie, the owner, is firing me. He says a married waitress isn't as reliable as a single one. He's already hired my replacement. I'm training her."

"What? A married girl works fine. Look at me and Allie. Thirty-five years we've been working together, side by side."

"Good years, all of them," said Allie.

"I want you to see the apartment and the office," I told Tracy.

"Yes," said Ben. "Take her to see them. I left them unlocked. I go back to helping Allie."

"Wait!" I said. "I just gave Tracy two kittens as a Christmas present. Are you OK with our having pets?"

Ben smiled. "Certainly. Who does not like pets?"

Tracy loved both the office and the apartment. We signed a lease for one year. As I wrote out the check I worried a little about my bank account. I had enough, but just barely.

"Move in when you want," Ben told us. "After you are man and wife. Tracy, when can you start work?"

"How about right after New Year's?"

"But your honeymoon?"

"We're putting it off until spring. We want to spend it on a dude ranch."

"Oh, what fun, with horses," cried Allie.

"January second, you start work. OK?" asked Ben.

"Deal!" said Tracy. We shook hands all around.

Back in the car, I talked Tracy into dropping by Lund's to pick up her car.

"I can drive fine. My ribs are hardly hurting."

"I can't believe it. I'm going to have a new job. And you're going to have a new office. And we're both going to have our own apartment together."

"Yeah, it's exciting. I just hope my check doesn't bounce."

"You've got the money Eben paid you."

"What money?"

"He slipped an envelope into your outside coat pocket."

"Why didn't you tell me that earlier?"

Eben's check was for more than it should have been, but I was glad to see it.

Christmas morning arrived and I had to go pick

up my girl and take her over to her folks for dinner. I wasn't looking forward to it, but it turned out to be better than I'd feared. The Clover's house was all slicked up for the holidays. There were hooked rugs on the floors, and afghans and doilies on all the furniture. Exotic and enticing smells came from the kitchen. There was a big elk roast.

"Shot it myself," boasted Jeremiah, Tracy's Pop. "One shot, through the brain."

"Oh?" I asked." Did you shoot it with a twenty-two?"

Jerry seemed offended. "No, a thirty-ought-six. An elk's a mighty big animal."

There was a goose, too. Rumor had it that Jerry killed it also. Probably with a bee-bee gun. There were mashed potatoes and yams, and rolls, and Jell-O, and apple strudel, and chocolate pie for desert. And enough gravy to float a good-sized kayak. The elk roast was great. Bing Crosby and Perry Como tried to out sing each other on the hi-fi.

It was just the five of us. Me, Tracy, Jerry, and Tracy's mom, Lilly. The fifth member was a guy identified only as Gramps. I don't know whose grandfather he was, but he didn't look like either Jerry or Lilly. He was a shrunken-up gnome with a head like a dried apple. He laughed a lot, for no particular reason, and spent a lot of time picking wax out of his ear with a his little finger. But for all his toothlessness and small size, he ate enough to satisfy a starving stevedore.

After chow, we groaned our way into the living

room and stared at the lit-up Christmas tree. There were presents for me and Tracy, though we'd asked them to not bother. We'd given them a big cheese box and a bottle of wine, which they loved. There was a frilly, fussy, nightgown for Tracy.

"For the honeymoon," said Lilly, blushing.

And there was a box of cigars for me. They were big cigars. I think they might have intimidated Winston Churchill.

"You can hand those out for celebrating newborn babies," Jerry said. "If they last that long." He gave me a huge wink, and refilled the eggnog glasses all around.

There was another package for me, from Tracy.

"You already gave me my present," I complained. I'd brought the gun to show the folks and they had whistled over its beauty and apparent potency. Tracy had dragged along the kittens, which she'd named Eben and Mayhew, and they had a great time batting at the Christmas ornaments.

"This is a special gift," said Tracy. "I got it for you last night."

I unwrapped the red-and-green present. Damned if it wasn't one of those ivory ibises the late Kirsten Lund had carved.

"It's for your collection," said Tracy. She turned to her folks. "Axe likes to collect a souvenir for every case he solves."

"Oh, it's beautiful," beamed Lilly. "What is it?"

"An Egyptian ibis," I said.

"I've shot those," piped up Gramps. I decided he must be Jerry's dad.

"I called Ollie Crampton last night," said Tracy. "I asked if I could buy it from him. He gave it to me."

"What's the material?" asked Jerry, tapping on the bird.

"The stuff that nightmares are made of," I said. "Merry Christmas, everyone."

END

If you have enjoyed this book, please go to its Amazon book page and leave a short review. It will be most appreciated!

OTHER BOOKS BY THIS AUTHOR:

DEAD MAN LIMPING
[ISBN: 978-1-940469-00-3]

When 1950s private eye Axel Hatchett is hired by a delectable redhead to turn up her missing husband, Hatchett discovers that the man is not only still alive, but is armed, probably crazy, and is on a killing spree that may include Hatchett! But something stinks about this case — big time — and it's not Hatchett's pet skunk, Ambrosia.

GLIMMER IN A GLASS EYE
[ISBN: 978-1-940469-02-7]

After 1950s gumshoe Axel Hatchett is hired to protect a used car dealer from a threat of murder, Hatchett finds himself in a nest of rattlesnakes — literally! When the car dealer is bumped off, and Hatchett's prime suspect is murdered, the sleuth is forced to sift through a deck of also-ran suspects to solve the two killings before another corpse is added. And to make matters worse, he's falling for a mouthy waitress who works in a sleazy diner....

SLAYER IN A GRAY TOUPEE
[ISBN: 978-1-940469-01-0]

Rumpled 1950s sleuth, Axel Hatchett, is summoned to the Flinders Mansion to prevent a millionaire's threatened murder. After a fierce blizzard knocks out the power and closes the roads, Hatchett is trapped in the candle-lit mansion with an eccentric array of terrified guests and servants. The detective is determined to solve the case, but his only clue is a sinister gray toupee.

KILLER BEAR FOR HIRE
[ISBN: 978-1-940469-04-1]

In all his years of sleuthing, snarky 1950s private eye Axel Hatchett has never faced a case like this: a bear trained to kill. Hatchett finds himself hunted by a deadly two-legged predator whose bullet comes unnervingly close to Hatchett's new wife, and that has Hatchett seeing red! Armed with a revolver and his caustic wits, Hatchett is out to solve a grizzly killing, or die trying.

BOOK CLUB DISCUSSION QUESTIONS
(For Those Who Didn't Succumb to the Curses)

1. Did the title lead you to expect a book about archeological digs, or about foul-mouthed women? Were you disappointed?

2. Do you think Tracy has it in her to become an operative?

3. All the books in this series have included death and snakes. Discuss what this means.

4. What themes does the author explore? (i.e., greed, jealousy, the backbiting nature of academics….)

5. What made you laugh? Did this lead to choking and necessitate the use of the Heimlich maneuver?

6. Was the ending satisfying? Were you hoping for more murders?

7. Would you call this a dystopian, or a utopian, novel? Explain.

8. Compare and contrast this book with other similar books you have read about the Egyptian god Thoth. Are there any?

9. Have you had any religious experiences while reading this book? Something to do with the Egyptian cat god, Bastet? My cat wants to know.

10. In the region where you live, are there any lost treasure stories? Do you have any favorite lost treasure stories you've heard or read about? Discuss.

ABOUT THE AUTHOR

Steven LeRoy Nelson is an award-winning humorist whose short fiction has appeared in *Alfred Hitchcock Mystery Magazine, Ellery Queen Mystery Magazine, The Leviathan,* and numerous other publications.

Visit him at his website at:

www.stevenleroynelson.com

www.ingramcontent.com/pod-product-compliance
Lightning Source LLC
Chambersburg PA
CBHW020417180626
46812CB00003B/1022